GENNIFER CHOLDENKO

PUFFIN BOOKS
An Imprint of Penguin Group (USA)

PUFFIN BOOKS
Published by the Penguin Group
Penguin Group (USA) LLC
375 Hudson Street
New York, New York 10014

USA * Canada * UK * Ireland * Australia
New Zealand * India * South Africa * China

penguin.com
A Penguin Random House Company

First published in the United States of America by Dial Books for Young Readers,
a division of Penguin Young Readers Group, 2013
Published by Puffin Books, an imprint of Penguin Young Readers Group, 2014

THE LIBRARY OF CONGRESS HAS CATALOGED THE DIAL BOOKS EDITION AS FOLLOWS:
Choldenko, Gennifer, date.
Al Capone does my homework / Gennifer Choldenko. p. cm.
Sequel to: Al Capone shines my shoes.
Summary: "Moose Flanagan, who lives on Alcatraz along with his family and the families of the other prison guards, faces new challenges when his father is promoted to associate warden"
—Provided by publisher.
Includes bibliographical references.
ISBN 978-0-8037-3472-2 (hardcover)
1. United States Penitentiary, Alcatraz Island, California—Juvenile fiction.
[1. United States Penitentiary, Alcatraz Island, California—Fiction.
2. Alcatraz Island (Calif.)—History—20th century—Fiction. 3. Swindlers and swindling—Fiction.
4. Fires—Fiction. 5. Autism—Fiction. 6. Brothers and sisters—Fiction.]
I. Title.
PZ7.C446265Akh 2013 [Fic]—dc23 2012039138

Puffin Books ISBN 978-0-14-242522-0

Printed in the United States of America

1 3 5 7 9 10 8 6 4 2

A little help from public enemy number one

On the top of the first page of my thesis about Roosevelt and his polio, it says *State problem* in handwriting that is hauntingly familiar.

Al Capone has sent me notes before. I know his handwriting really well.

But how did he get his hands on my homework? It must have been the cons who are working on our place. Somebody took my homework and gave it to him.

Except why'd he write that? *He* doesn't like my thesis? He's my English teacher now?

And then on the bottom of the last page he wrote:

Roosevelt is a good fella, but Capone is the guy you should be writing about. Okay, Roosevelt had a polio problem, but he was born rich. Capone started with nothing. He earned every penny himself.

Capone messed up my homework. How strange is that? A gangster did my homework. Not just any gangster, either—public enemy number one.

Luckily, he wrote in pencil.

OTHER BOOKS YOU MAY ENJOY

Al Capone Does My Shirts	Gennifer Choldenko
Al Capone Shines My Shoes	Gennifer Choldenko
The Boy Who Saved Baseball	John H. Ritter
The Cat Ate My Gymsuit	Paula Danziger
Emma-Jean Lazarus Fell Out of a Tree	Lauren Tarshis
A Long Way from Chicago	Richard Peck
Mockingbird	Kathryn Erskine
No Passengers Beyond This Point	Gennifer Choldenko
Notes from a Liar and Her Dog	Gennifer Choldenko
Over the Wall	John H. Ritter
Travel Team	Mike Lupica
A Year Down Yonder	Richard Peck

To my dad,

James Alexander Johnson

Table of Contents

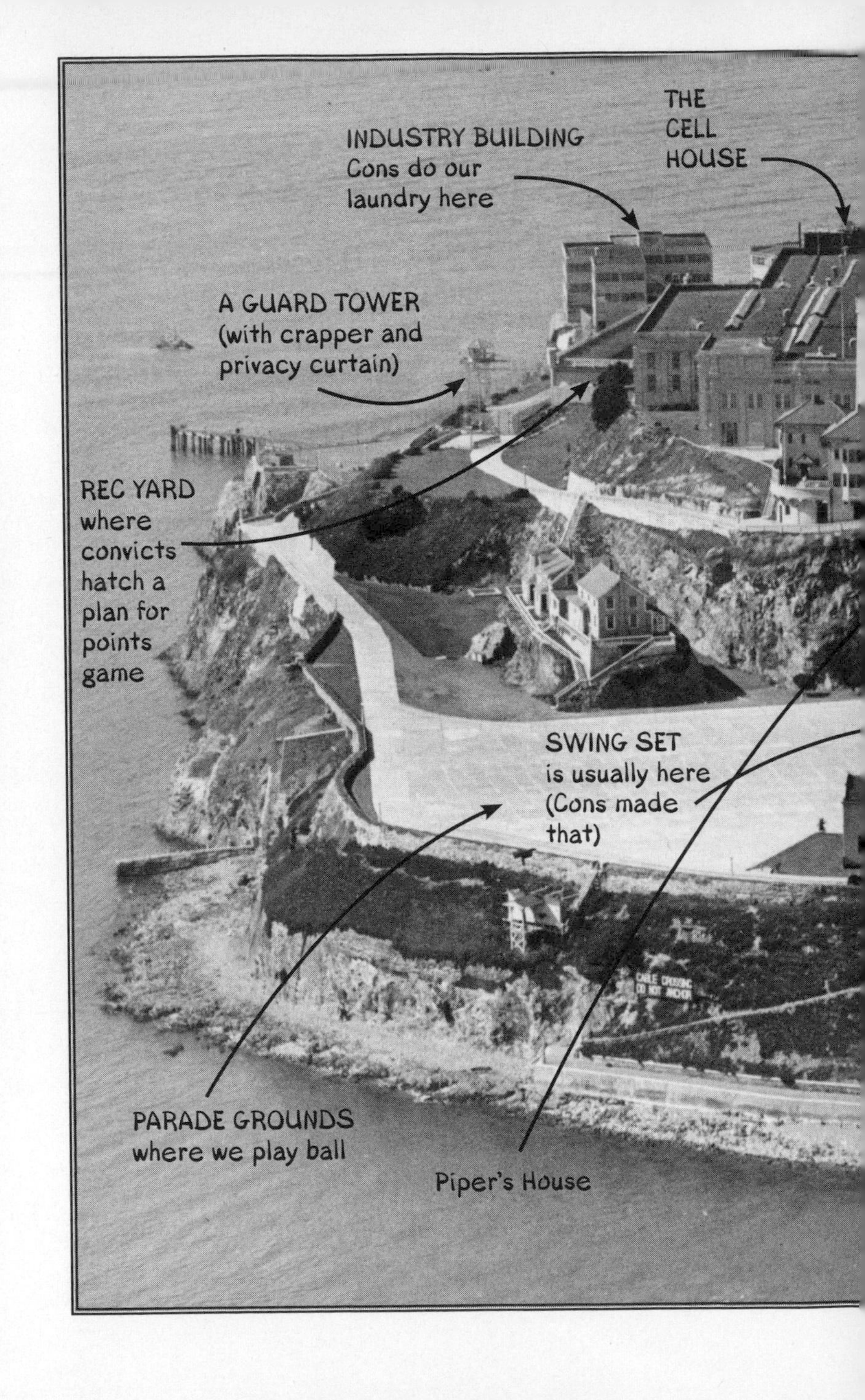
THE
CELL
HOUSE
INDUSTRY BUILDING
Cons do our
laundry here
A GUARD TOWER
(with crapper and
privacy curtain)
REC YARD
where
convicts
hatch a
plan for
points
game
SWING SET
is usually here
(Cons made
that)
PARADE GROUNDS
where we play ball
Piper's House

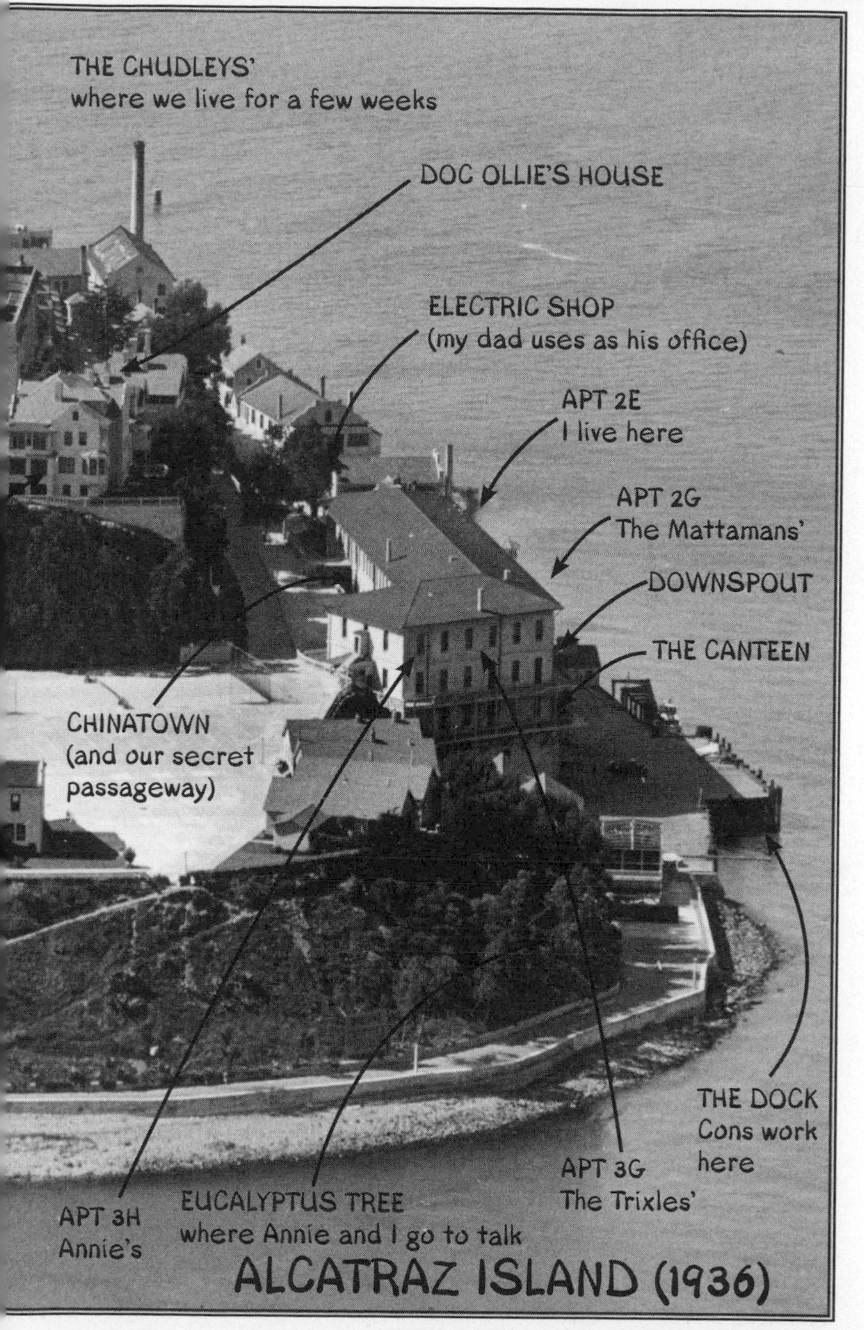

San Francisco History Center, San Francisco Public Library

1. The Warden's Son

Sunday, January 19, 1936

Today is my dad's first official day as associate warden on Alcatraz Island, home to anyone who is anyone in the criminal world. On our island we have world-famous robbers, thieves, swindlers, sharpshooters, second-story burglars, mad-dog murderers, plus a whole lot of ordinary criminals—vicious but not well-known.

No one ever believes I live on Alcatraz. Even my eighth-grade history teacher made me write on the chalkboard *I do not live on Alcatraz* two hundred times. She didn't even apologize when she found out I wasn't lying.

My mother couldn't buy stockings at O'Connor and Moffat's. They wouldn't take her check, on account of it said: *Helen Flanagan, Alcatraz Island, California*. My father had trouble getting his driver's license. They thought he was an escaped prisoner too stupid to fake his address, instead of an officer at the most notorious prison in North America.

My friend Annie was kicked out of Sunday school for saying she lived on Alcatraz. They sent her to confession. She confessed she didn't live on Alcatraz and the next day she confessed she'd lied in confession.

Of course, Piper, the warden's daughter, never gets in trouble for anything. Nothing sticks to her. She's as slippery as a bar of soap.

I'm betting a guard like Darby Trixle—also known as Double Tough—doesn't have these kinds of problems either. Darby was born in a uniform, one size too tight. My dad, on the other hand, looks like a middle-age dance instructor. You'd never expect him to carry a firearm. An accordion maybe, but not a rifle. Not that there are firearms everywhere on Alcatraz. Only up in the guard towers and the catwalks. At any given moment you are in the crosshairs down at the dock, but not up on the parade grounds.

My dad may not look the part, but as of today, he's the number two guy on the island. Piper lords it over all the kids that she's the warden's daughter, but now I'm the *warden's son*. Okay, the associate warden . . . but still.

In the kitchen, Dixieland band music is playing on the radio and my father is dressed in his crisp blue uniform. My mom is patiently trying to brush my sixteen-year-old sister Natalie's hair, which she really hates.

From a distance Nat seems normal, but when you get close you start to notice things are a bit off. She rocks from side to side. She drags her chin along her chest. She won't ever look in your eyes, and sometimes stares straight at your privates. My dad says Natalie views the world through her own personal kaleidoscope and it's our job to see from her perspective. That sounds good until she's counting every hairpin in the bathroom when my bladder is about to explode, or she's lying flat on the ground in the middle of the train station when the cutest girl in school walks by.

Today, Mom and Nat are waiting for Mrs. Kelly to arrive.

Mrs. Kelly is the teacher who helps her learn the social graces.

"You nervous?" I ask my father as he sits on the edge of his bed, giving his shoes a last buff. His face is newly shaved, his skin smells of soap, and his shoes are as shiny as good silver spoons, but still he keeps shining them.

"He's fine," my mother calls.

My father smiles as he slips his stocking feet into his shoes. "See, I'm fine," he says, smoothing down his hair and placing his officer's cap squarely on his head.

"You're nervous," I say.

"Could be," he answers.

"You want one of Nat's buttons . . . for luck?" Natalie collects buttons. She loves them the way I love baseball.

"Think she could spare one?"

I head back to the kitchen. "Nat, Dad needs a button. Can you let him have one?"

Nat's head is down, inches from her plate, her eyes focused on chasing the slippery whites of her egg. My mother glares at me. "I just got her to sit down for breakfast."

Nat wiggles out of her chair and heads into the living room. A minute later she comes back with her hand tightly closed.

She walks up to my dad, who is gulping the last of his coffee, and opens her fist to reveal one flat, four-hole button.

My father beams at her. "That's a beaut, sweet pea," he says, sliding it into his pocket.

"Ninety-seven," Nat says.

"I'll take good care of ninety-seven. You betcha. Guess I'm all set now, except for one thing." He gives my mother an embarrassingly long kiss.

My mom smiles. "Good luck," she says.

I follow him outside. He grins at me. "Where do you think you're going? Think I can't handle the job on my own, do you?"

"Of course you can handle it," I say, though I am worried. My dad is too nice to be a warden.

I watch as he walks across the connecting balconies and turns the corner to the stairs. A minute later, he's down below, where eight cons are sweeping the dock. Darby Trixle's got his eye on them, barking orders through his bullhorn. He loves that bullhorn, sleeps with it under his pillow. Probably takes it to the bathroom with him too. I can just hear him: "Bowel movement approaching."

I follow along after my dad down the stairs. Not close enough for him to notice. I don't want him to send me back home.

"Good morning, Darby." My father walks over for a chat.

Darby sucks his belly in and pokes his chest out. "Good morning, boss," he says.

Will Darby be nice to me now that my dad is his boss?

Probably not.

My dad looks at all the prisoners as he talks to Darby. I know the names of some. There's #227, Lizard, a big woolly mammoth of a guy with a puffy face and spindly legs. Annie says he ate a lizard in the rec yard once—that's how he got his name. There's #300, Count Lustig, a world-famous con man. And there's #141, Indiana, who has no chin and no eyebrows. Indiana waves at me when Darby isn't looking. But having a chinless, eyebrow-less felon wave at you is not fun, believe me.

I'm not the only guy watching all of this either. Donny

Caconi is on the 64 building phone, but his eyes are tracking the cons. Donny is the grown son of Mrs. Caconi, the lady who knocks on your door if the phone is for you. Since she weighs more than a river barge, and there are a lot of steps in 64 building, this is impressive. Mrs. Caconi's husband used to be a guard here, but he got transferred and she didn't go with him. Nobody knows why.

Donny is tall, thin, and graceful as a girl—the opposite of his mother—and he dresses snappy like he has loads of girlfriends. He nods his head at me as if I'm his long-lost friend. Donny is everybody's long-lost friend. We all really like him.

Dad finishes his conversation and heads up the switchback.

Then I see Count Lustig motion to Darby. Darby rolls his eyes at the Count but walks his way. With Darby's back turned, Indiana spits on the dock behind my father. Lizard and another con with red hair laugh.

My father glances back at them, his brow furrowed. He knows something happened, but he's not sure what. He's too far up the road to do anything anyway . . . but I'm not.

A little voice in my head tells me this is not my business and I should stay out of it. But that little voice doesn't understand how I'm the warden's son now, and I have to start acting like it.

My feet step over the white painted line that we're not supposed to cross when the cons are down here.

"Don't do that!" I tell Indiana in my most threatening voice, but I'm so nervous, it comes out wibbly-wobbly.

Indiana looks at me with his chinless, eyebrow-less face. Lizard cocks his head toward Indiana as if to say *Take a look at that kid*.

Darby half walks, half runs toward me, his tight blue officer's jacket bristling. "Get outta here." He waves me back in short angry motions.

"He spit at my father," I say. But when I look at Indiana, his face is perfectly blank, like he doesn't speak our language.

"Your father needs his kid to take care of him?" Trixle barks.

"He didn't see it. I did."

Trixle shakes his head, then waggles his finger at me. "I don't care what you see. You stay out of the dock area when the cons are down here, because I sure as heck don't need your help."

My arms are shaking and my legs feel like tapioca pudding. I retreat back across the line as fast as my shaky legs will take me.

2. America's Roughest Prison

Sunday, January 19, 1936

"Darby's a blowhard. Just ignore him," Donny says when he catches up to me on the parade grounds—a big cement area in the middle level of the island where we play ball and roller skate and stuff.

Donny came up here just to talk to me?

Donny hasn't forgotten what it's like to be a kid, the way most grown-ups have. I wish he lived here all the time, but at least he visits a couple of days a week to get his laundry done. On Alcatraz, the convicts do our laundry, except for Mrs. Caconi's. She doesn't want convicts touching her clothes. But Donny doesn't care. He doesn't mind who does his laundry, so long as it isn't him.

"Darby bugs me," I say.

Donny nods. "Darby's a piece of work. He's got his sights on your dad. He was sure that job was his."

This is what I think too, but having an adult tell me in so many words . . . that's another thing entirely.

"You keep an eye out. He's a good man, your father, and I wouldn't want anything to happen to him."

"Wh-what are you worried will happen?"

"He's in a tight spot is all. He's got the cons on one side

testing him. And Darby on the other hankering for his job." Donny angles his hat over one eye. If my father tried that, he'd look silly. Donny Caconi never looks silly.

"Moose." My mom waves me down, half running toward us from the back side of 64 building. "I need you home."

"Now? I've only been gone for five minutes."

Donny gives me a sly smile. "I got a mother like that. Drives you crazy, doesn't it?"

It's so good to hear him say this. He knows just how I feel.

"Better step to it. You know she isn't going to give up until she has you where she wants you."

When I get back to #2E, Nat is in the bathroom flushing the toilet once, twice, three times. Natalie goes to the Esther P. Marinoff, a boarding school for kids who are unusual the way she is. But, most weekends she gets to come home, and then I'm responsible for her.

"Natalie," I yell, "quit it."

The flushing stops and she moves to her favorite part of every room: the light switch. On-off, on-off. She'll stand there until next Christmas if you let her.

"No funny business," Mrs. Kelly says. Mrs. Kelly is the size of a gnome compared to my mom, who is tall and graceful. Nat comes out of the bathroom and begins to rock from one foot to the other, exploring her lip with her teeth.

"We need your help with the eye contact situation," Mrs. Kelly informs me. She never says hello or how are you. She just launches right in with what she wants you to do. For a person who is supposed to teach the social graces, she is pretty darn abrupt.

Just once I wish she'd ask about me and not only about Natalie. It's like I have *Natalie's brother* tattooed to my forehead.

"We have to work twice as hard now, Moose. Natalie's the warden's daughter. She can't call attention to herself. She has to learn to blend in," my mom says.

Natalie blend in? Is she joking? "Doesn't Nat work on eye contact at school?" I offer.

"She's off this week, so I thought we could use this opportunity to work on this at home. You are such a nice young man. I knew you'd help us." Mrs. Kelly smiles as if I've already agreed.

Donny Caconi just got through telling me I need to watch out for my dad. How am I supposed to take care of him and Natalie too?

My mom's eyes are drilling into me. Clearly I'm not leaving here until I do what they want.

"Something with math," I suggest. "We could make flash cards with long numbers written on them and hold them above our eyes. Natalie would have to look at the numbers while we're talking. She'd get used to looking at people's eyes rather than at their shoes."

Mrs. Kelly nods at my mother, then looks back to me. "Get her in the habit . . . is that it?"

"Yeah, maybe we can, you know, get her interested in counting eyebrow hairs or something."

Mrs. Kelly doesn't crack a smile. She has the sense of humor of a fire hydrant. "Flash cards might work." She nods. "Want to give it a go?"

"Me?"

Mrs. Kelly nods emphatically. "You've got a way with her, Moose."

"Yeah, but . . ."

Mrs. Kelly's nostrils flare. "Unless you can't be bothered."

"It might not work," I respond lamely.

"Listen to me, you are more important to Natalie than anyone else. . . you know that, don't you?"

"No, I'm not," I say.

My mother is avoiding my eyes. Maybe I should put a card on my forehead for *her*.

DON'T DO THIS TO ME it would say.

"How old are you?" Mrs. Kelly asks.

"Thirteen."

"I'm sixty-two. Your mother is what?" Mrs. Kelly turns to my mother.

"Thirty-eight."

"You do the math, Moose. You're going to know Natalie her whole life. We won't."

"What's that supposed to mean?" I mumble as I watch Natalie. She's rolled up in her favorite purple blanket, which is what she does when she gets upset.

"It means you'll be around when we're not," Mrs. Kelly says in a voice tough as gristle.

"Look. I'll do my best, but Natalie has to try. I can't make her."

"This is important for her. She has to learn this." Mrs. Kelly doesn't even seem to hear me.

"I said I'd try," I say. "Could I be excused now?" I pounce on the door like it's a piece of chocolate cake.

My mom barely moves her head, but I take it as a yes. The

door bangs behind me and I scoot across the balconies, up the stairs, to the switchback.

I'm headed for the warden's house. Piper isn't my favorite person on the island, but her father's been a warden her whole life. He was at San Quentin before this and some other prison before that. She'll know what I should do to watch my dad's back.

The warden's house is a twenty-two-room mansion at the tiptop of the island. It smells like roses, and I can hear the sound of a violin concerto coming through the open window—as if it's on Broadway Street in Pacific Heights instead of thirty feet from the most notorious cell house in North America. I take a deep breath to calm down before knocking.

"Moose!" The warden answers the door in the three-piece suit that he wears like a uniform, his baby Walter in his arms. Even with a blue baby blanket wrapped over his shoulder, the warden is his own kind of scary.

"Why, if it isn't young Mr. Flanagan, Walty." The warden waves the baby's hand at me. "Say hi to Mr. Flanagan."

"Umm hi, Walty." I wave back stupidly.

"Big day for the Flanagan family," the warden says. "Think you can handle the responsibility?"

"Me?" My voice comes out strange, like I've sucked the air out of a balloon.

"Who else would I mean, Mr. Flanagan?" the warden asks.

"Yes, sir," I mumble.

"Your dad is going to make a good warden, you know why?" The warden taps the side of his skull. "He's a thinker. You take a page from his book and you'll be fine. Piper can give you a few tips," he says as Piper comes down the stairs like she's the queen or something. Her long dark hair is in a ponytail tied with a red bow. She has on a red blouse with her old overalls. There's just something about Piper . . . She makes other girls look like yesterday's tuna fish. I think I'm over her and then I see her and I know I'm not.

We go through the large dining room to their huge kitchen with the brand-spanking-new stuff like an electric icebox and an electric mixer. Rich people don't even need to mix their own cake batter. It's amazing.

Piper motions for me to sit down at the kitchen table, then follows suit, sighing dramatically. "So you need something, is that it?"

My cheeks flush. She's kind of right. I do only come up here when I need something. The trouble with Piper is I like her outsides, but not her insides.

"Just looking for some advice on how to keep an eye on my dad."

"Well . . . I don't know if you're ready to hear about that," she says.

"Of course I'm ready."

She shrugs. "I've noticed that your priorities are confused."

"Which means?" I ask.

"All you want to do is play baseball with Annie."

"*You* don't play baseball."

"I'm just saying if you want to be friends with me, you have to act like it."

"What about you? At school, you never even give me the time of day," I say.

"I'm not talking about at school."

"What *are* you talking about?"

"Here on the island. A little gift here and there, like flowers, say . . ." She holds her index finger in the air, like I should wait, trots out the kitchen door, then comes back with a gold gift box.

She lifts off the box top. "This is from my secret admirer."

Inside is a fuzzy turquoise sweater.

"Who gave you that?"

She snorts. "I just told you. It's from my secret admirer."

"But you must have some idea who it is."

"Secret. Don't you get it?" She rubs the sweater. "I'm only showing you as an example of the kind of thing that gets a girl's attention."

"Oh, I see. This is to help me," I say sarcastically.

"Some people know how to treat girls, that's all. I mean, something like this makes you loyal. How do you think Al Capone does it?"

Alphonse Capone, Alcatraz #85, is the most famous gangster in America—maybe even the world. Anybody who finds out I live on Alcatraz always wants to know if I've met Al Capone. Warden Williams calls him *our star boarder*.

"First off, how can you be loyal to your secret admirer if you don't even know who he is?"

"When I find out, I will be."

"Why are you modeling yourself after Al Capone, anyway?" I ask.

"People love him. They'll do anything for him."

"He buys them," I say.

"You should see the letters he gets."

I roll my eyes.

"Look, it's tricky business being the warden's kid. And I'm

the only one who can show you how it's done. So I would be a lot nicer to me if I were you."

"Fine." My hands fly up. "I get it."

She smiles. "All right then. I'll tell you. Chudley . . . you're familiar with Chudley, aren't you?"

Man, I hate when she does this. She knows I know the latest gossip about former Associate Warden Chudley. "Yes," I say.

"If your father cooperates with the cons, like Chudley did, he'll get fired."

"Are you kidding me? My father would never do that. How is being a warden any different than being a guard? The guards could cooperate with the cons too, you know."

"A guard can only do so much. Wardens have power. I mean, who's going to stop a warden?"

"How does your father handle it?"

"He's been tested. They know he can't be broken. But your dad . . ."

"They know my dad too."

"Men behave differently when they're in charge. Will he be fair or play favorites?" She nods, then breathes in like she's about to swim a long distance underwater. "How will he deal with the games?"

"Games? What are you talking about?"

She has a piece of paper in her hand, which she sets down in front of me like it's the Declaration of Independence. I read the neat printing.

Spitting on a guard = 5
Spitting on a warden = 20
Making a shiv = 40

Stealing a knife = 50
Stabbing a guard = 250
Stabbing a warden = 500
Death Bonus: guard = 1,000
Death Bonus: warden = 5,000

"These are the points the cons get. And how do you get the most points?" She thumps the page.

"Kill a warden."

"How many wardens are there?" She holds up two fingers like she's my nursery school teacher. "Two. Your dad and mine."

I'm about to tell Piper what Indiana did, but I stop myself. I don't want her to know that Indiana got twenty points off my father on his first morning. "What do they get if they win?"

"A title. The toughest guy at the roughest hard-time prison in America. You know, like America's heavyweight champion."

"That's nothing to be proud of."

"That's what I think. That's what you think. It's not what they think."

I squint at her. "You made this up."

"No." She smoothes the page. "This showed up on the steam table in the convict cafeteria."

"Can't your dad do anything?"

"What's he going to do . . . this is the end of the line. Alcatraz is the prison other wardens send their troublemakers to."

"Does my dad know about this?"

"Of course. Look . . ." She takes a deep theatrical breath. "All I'm saying is . . . this is way more important than baseball."

"Yeah, okay, but I can't follow my dad around all the time."

"I'll know what's going on. Stick close"—she shakes her finger at me—"and you'll know too."

"How do you find out?"

"I have ears. My father doesn't like his cell house office. He prefers working here."

I know what she's saying is crucial. I need to protect my father. That *is* more important than anything else. But there's something about Piper that always makes me feel like I have a fishhook in my belly and she has the pole in her hand.

3. Explosion

Sunday, January 19, 1936

It's lucky I finished my paper on President Roosevelt, because it's due tomorrow and now I have to babysit. It's pretty unusual that I finished early. The last time I did anything early was when I was born and I came out three weeks before I was due.

I even did a good job on the paper. My thesis is *Overcoming polio helped President Roosevelt become the man he is today*. It wasn't that bad to write, either. I enjoyed my homework? Okay, now I'm starting to sound scary. Pretty soon I'll be talking about the wonders of Brussels sprouts and how hygiene is fun, fun, fun!

Tonight my parents are going out with Warden Williams and his wife to celebrate my father's first day as associate warden. I can hear Nat in the kitchen, opening the icebox. She likes to make sandwiches, but when she's done the kitchen looks like the *Titanic* after the iceberg. Now she takes her sandwich into my room and gets the light switch plate all sticky from her jammy hands as she stands there turning the lights on and off, on and off.

I head for the kitchen to assess the damage, just as Theresa Mattaman knocks and then comes in the front door. At eight years old, Theresa doesn't get the part about asking permission. Her knock lets you know she's about to barge in.

Theresa's black curly hair is messy as usual, and she's wearing her pajamas. She never takes them off—not for school, not for church, not for anything—she just piles her clothes over the top. If you look closely, you can always see a little pajama sticking out somewhere. Theresa lives with her two brothers—Baby Rocky and my buddy Jimmy, who is almost thirteen.

I'm blasting cold water and rubbing a chip of ice on my itchy skin. I get hives when I get anxious. Apparently being the warden's son makes me nervous.

"Where's Nat?" Theresa asks.

"In my room."

She nods and trots off to find her.

I put the ice chip on the counter and open the bread box. Nothing like a sandwich to make me feel better. I'll clean up the kitchen later. I'm spreading the mayo when Theresa hops into the kitchen again.

"I have a message from Piper," she announces.

Normally, Theresa and Piper get along like a pocket full of firecrackers. "Since when are you Piper's messenger girl?" I ask.

Theresa wiggles her finger like I should come closer. "She pays me. I do whatever she wants now."

"Really?"

Theresa responds with a bouncy-curls nod. "Sometimes she buys me things. Really good stuff too, like licorice and root beer . . . You should get on her payroll."

"There's an idea . . . What's the message?" I ask.

"Don't forget the flowers." Theresa's voice drops to a whisper. "Are you sweet on her, Moose? Are you? Or is it

Annie? I won't tell. I promise." She motions like she's buttoning her lips.

"I'm not sweet on anybody," I say.

"That's what I told them."

"Who is them?"

"Annie and Jimmy. They said while I was delivering my message I should find out." Theresa beckons with her finger. "But mostly they want to know if you're going to be different now that you're a warden's kid."

"What?"

"Annie says you'll worry more. And Jimmy says you might get bossy."

I open the butter dish, but there are teeth marks where Nat has taken a bite out of the cube. I cover the butter so Theresa won't see.

"Is Theresa in there?" Annie calls through the screen door.

"Yes," I answer.

Theresa gives me a sour look, like I'm a cell house snitch, but I'm not going to lie to Annie. Annie's my best friend who is a girl.

"Come on in, Annie. And by the way, I'm not going to be any different."

Annie's face turns emergency red. Since her hair is white blond and her skin is so light, when she blushes, you can see from a mile away. She's gotten a lot taller the last few months and more, you know, girlish. And her arm is stronger. She's always been a great pitcher, but I swear she pitches even faster now.

"I know you're not," she says. "I just don't want your dad's new job to interfere with baseball."

"*Nothing* interferes with baseball."

"Glad to hear it. C'mon, Theresa, your mom says it's time for bed."

Theresa's shoulders droop.

"You can't stay? You just got here," I tell Annie.

"I know, I'm sorry. Mrs. Mattaman sent me to get Theresa. It's past her bedtime."

"You've been at the Mattamans'?"

Annie nods. "But I have to go home now."

"You sure?"

"Sure I'm sure."

I stand watching as Annie and Theresa walk down the balcony to the Mattamans'. I'm still watching after they go inside.

Natalie brings her blankets into my room and sets up her buttons, my books, and my toothbrush. She loves my toothbrush. Who knows why? Then she goes back to work on the light switch. On-off. On-off.

I'm tired, but I don't like to fall asleep when I'm babysitting Natalie. I rearrange the pillows to get my head in a comfortable position. Then I prop a pillow against the wall and scoot myself up, but I keep slipping down again. The next thing I know, I'm dreaming of a campfire. The fire is crackling. My marshmallows are a golden brown sagging off the stick.

I'm trying to think if I've ever had a dream so vivid I could smell it, when my hand bumps against the edge of the pillow and touches something hot. Wait, the wall is hot! I bolt out of bed, then fly to the bedroom door. Didn't I leave that open? Are my parents home? I wrap my fingers around the burning hot doorknob.

The smoke billows in.

"Natalie!" I shout, "Come on!" She's burrowed into her blankets on my floor. I grab her arm, but she forces her hands farther underneath her, jamming her face deep into the pillow.

"Natalie!" The smoke burns my eyes. My throat stings like pins pricking it.

I cough, trying to snatch the pillow.

"I don't like the smell," she mumbles, her voice muffled by bedclothes.

I try to hoist her over my shoulder. She's older than I am but a good thirty pounds lighter. I've carried her before, only now her body is stiff as a stadium bleacher.

"Buttons," Natalie says.

I grip her beloved button box and push through the doorway.

The smoke is getting blacker, denser. I suck it down my throat and up my nostrils as I half carry, half drag Natalie clutching her pillow, her legs bumping behind us. Through the living room we go, dodging licks of fire. My eyes smart, I can hardly see, but now that Nat has her buttons, she's letting me move her.

The flames have engulfed the front door. How do we get out?

Maybe I can use the side table to break the window, but I'll need to let go of Natalie.

"Natalie . . . don't move!" Her legs are so stiff, it's as if rigor mortis has set in. She lies on the ground as she did on my floor, her head face-first in the pillow.

Wait . . . this isn't stupid, it's smart. She's protecting herself from the smoke. It's less dense down low. The thoughts spin in my brain as I hammer the side table against the glass. The windows are thick, they won't break. But something is cracking. The other window. The fire must have popped the glass, but the flames are too hot over there. We can't get out that way.

I batter the window with the table, pummel it as hard as I can and then a splintering snap and the glass shatters around me, leaving a jagged sharp-sided hole.

I still have hold of the table leg, reeling it back through the broken glass and setting the table down in front of the window. "Natalie, climb!" I shout.

She freezes—won't move at all. Her head is burrowed in the pillow, her arms clutching her button box. I snatch the pillow from her.

"Come on!" With more strength than I thought I had, I pick her up and put her on the table.

But this isn't going to work. How can I get her through the window? The smoke is slowing my brain. It takes a long time to reason this out.

The flames bust out of the kitchen, creating a wall of heat behind us. A hot rush of fire-fueled air whirls around us, sparks shooting, singeing my arm.

Then all of a sudden she dives through the jagged glass and I'm on her tail. I jump through, landing in a jumble on top of her.

"Fire!" somebody cries.

"Fire! Fire!" More yells from all around.

"Moose!" Mrs. Mattaman appears out of the smoke, her apron soaking wet, her dark eyes black with fear. She grasps my arm. "You okay?"

"Yes," I tell her, but I'm not sure the word makes it out of my throat, though it must have, because she nods.

"Jesus, what happened?" Donny Caconi's voice rings in from the night as a sudden shock of cold water blasts from below.

Natalie shudders until it finally registers in my brain that I'm holding on to her and I should let go. Nat hates to be touched.

I stare stupidly at the flames exploding out of our apartment. I can't believe this is happening.

4. The Flanagan Girl

Sunday, January 19, 1936

The balcony vibrates with boots marching up and down the stairs. Water slops our feet. Buckets clank, hoses spray a fine mist on our heads.

Officer Trixle has his bullhorn and he's belting out orders while standing under the balcony light. "Get the kids outta here. Aim that away. Hot spots in the kitchen." Mr. Bomini is on the front of the bucket brigade, pouring water on the fire while Mr. Mattaman operates the hose.

Where are my parents? What time is it? Shouldn't they be home? The last ferry is at 11:30.

I can't stop shivering or keep my teeth from chattering. Nat is hunkered down next to me like an inanimate object. She doesn't even seem to want her button box, which I'm surprised to see in my hand. I hardly remember grabbing it.

Mrs. Mattaman gives me a gentle push. She has Baby Rocky, who is a year old, in her arms, his head buried in her chest. "Go on down now," she tells me.

We're in the way up here, but so far I've been unable to get Nat to move. Sometimes she hunkers down and there's nothing you can do.

"Nat, come on," I tell her gently. I can see Piper with baby Walty, Annie, Theresa, and Jimmy all standing together at the foot of the dock guard tower, a safe distance away from everything. I want to join them in the worst way. But Nat is so upset, she's stopped listening. Nothing I say seems to have any effect.

Finally, when I've given up trying, Nat pops up and begins toe-walking across the balcony and down the stairs.

I try to steer her toward everyone. Her head is hanging, her attention on her feet.

"Moose!" Theresa practically jumps at me. "Are you okay?"

"Moose!" Annie gives me a hug and then seems to realize what she's doing and stops. "What happened?"

I shake my head. "I dunno."

"Didn't I tell you being a warden's kid is harder than it looks," Piper whispers in my ear.

Slowly her words sink in. Could she be right? Could this have something to do with my dad's promotion? My stomach feels like a popped balloon.

Jimmy is peering at me. "You hungry?" he asks.

I nod. I am always hungry.

He digs in his pocket for a couple of smashed-up cookies in waxed paper. We all huddle together, eating cookie crumbs and watching guards fight the fire. Annie is holding baby Walty. Piper sent Theresa up the hill to the warden's house to get diapers and then back up again for a bottle.

Officers work under the floodlights, manning dock hoses and shuttling water hand over hand in bucket brigades from neighboring apartments. An officer in his bathrobe pulls our kitchen chair out of the apartment and hoses it down. Officers in shirtsleeves smother the blaze with rugs and blankets.

"Get out of the way. Turn the hose up. Hot spots back there," Trixle shouts, his voice hoarse even with the bullhorn. For once, I'm glad for that bullhorn.

"Where are your parents?" Annie whispers.

I shrug. "They went to the yacht club to have dinner with the warden. I thought they'd be home by now."

"My parents aren't back either," Piper says.

"That must have been so scary," Annie says, "trying to get Natalie out."

I don't say anything. I don't want to talk about how scary it was.

Slowly the crackling roar dies down, the wall of heat lifts, and the cool of the evening returns. Puddles, empty buckets, and axes litter the dock. The island truck is parked cockeyed with one door open. Several hoses are crisscrossed between 64 building and the bay.

I don't know how long we stand like this, but my parents still aren't back and Annie and her dad have gone into the city. He burned his hand. Must have been bad too, because Doc Ollie sent him all the way to San Francisco Hospital instead of treating him here.

My feet are numb by the time the men straggle down the 64 building stairs. Mr. Mattaman's face is grimy and he's missing his uniform jacket. Officer Trixle's hair is black with ash. He's in his shirtsleeves, his chest puffed up and his muscled arms shiny with sweat as he holds the bullhorn to his lips. With my father and the warden off the island, he's senior officer and he wants everybody to know it.

"All clear," he bellows. "Go on now. You folks go home."

I look up at my home. The windows are shattered, revealing a blackened hole inside. There's a mess of buckets on the balcony and black scorch marks on the wall.

All I can think of is my baseball glove. If it burned up, I'll never replace that. It was worn in just the way I like it.

Then I look at Natalie. I'm glad we have her button box, but we don't have my toothbrush or her favorite purple blanket. Did they burn too? I feel bad thinking about possessions when Annie's dad's hand got hurt, but I can't help it.

"You going to be okay, Moose?" Piper asks, surprising me with the softness in her voice.

"Yeah," I say, though my head feels like a few hundred cars have driven through it.

"I gotta get Walty to bed," Piper tells me.

I watch as she heads up the switchback.

"Where you gonna go, Moose?" Theresa asks.

"He's coming home with us," Jimmy announces.

"Natalie!" Theresa claps her hands. "You can sleep in my room. Won't that be fun?" she asks as we trudge to 64, past a small group of adults.

"The least they could do was build us a fire escape," Bea Trixle, Darby's wife, complains. Her hair is white blond, but black at the roots. She's wearing a uniform shirt of Darby's with her skirt and high heels. "It's a death trap, our 64 building. Might as well get some barbeque sauce and call it a day. How did it start, anyway?"

"Just what I was wondering," Donny Caconi says as he

stacks the extra buckets, his dungarees wet at the bottom and dusted with ash.

"Ask Moose." Darby nods toward me.

"Do you know, Moose?" Bea's voice is tight as a stretched rubber band.

I think about the flames shooting out from the kitchen. "I have no idea."

"It was *her,* wasn't it." Bea points her head toward Natalie. "She was counting matches or some fool thing."

"No!" I say.

Bea's face is red and puffy, and her arms are wrapped around her seven-year-old daughter, Janet, protecting her as if the fire is still raging.

"Could have burned the whole place down, killed every last one of us," Darby Trixle says. "Look at her. She can't even look at me. That's a guilty girl if ever I saw one."

We all stare at Natalie, who is picking at her chest with her chin.

"She didn't do this. Just because she's different, doesn't mean she's guilty." I try hard to speak gently and reasonably the way my father would.

Officer Trixle looks up at our apartment and then back around to the dark water behind us. There's no moonlight tonight, only the fog closing in like a lid. Mrs. Caconi stands huddled in her giant pink bathrobe.

"I always liked you, Moose, but don't try to protect your sister." Bea shakes her finger at me. Janet watches, her eyes dazed. She hasn't left her mother's side all evening.

"It wasn't Natalie," I tell her.

"How do you know?" Darby asks.

"Because I was there."

"But you were asleep, weren't you?" Darby asks.

"Natalie was asleep," my mouth says, while my head tells me what a chump I am. If I'd stayed awake, none of this would have happened.

Bea's chin is raised. "How do you know that?"

"Now look here, Bea," Mrs. Mattaman jumps in. "This isn't the time or place for this. We'll sort it out in the morning."

"I got a right to know where the Flanagan girl is sleeping tonight," Bea Trixle says, her hands on her hips.

"I'd like to know that too," Mrs. Caconi joins in. Some of the other folks from 64 building nod their heads.

"They're sleeping at our apartment," Theresa says.

"Oh, my. I think I have a migraine coming on," Mrs. Caconi says, tightening the belt of her bathrobe.

"C'mon Mama, you'll feel better when you lie down." Donny puts his arm around her and walks with her back to the Caconis' apartment.

Bea Trixle's eyes find Mrs. Mattaman. "The Flanagan girl is staying with you, Anna Maria?" she asks.

I don't think Jimmy and Theresa consulted her; still Mrs. Mattaman doesn't skip a beat. "That's the plan."

"Who's going to keep watch, then?" Bea has her nose right up in Mrs. Mattaman's face.

"Keep watch?" I ask.

"So's she don't burn the rest of the building down," Bea says.

Donny is back outside now, without his mom. "I'm sure there's another explanation for how the fire started," he says.

Darby scowls at him. "I doubt it."

"Could be an electrical fire," Donny offers.

"In the electrician's apartment?" Bea Trixle asks.

"Old rags soaked with cleaning fluid or linseed oil. Old wiring on the stove. Could have been a lot of things," Donny tells her.

"Cam runs a loose ship. Can't even control his own kids. I been saying that all along," Darby snarls.

I glare at him, pushing away the thoughts of Nat making sandwiches by herself.

She wouldn't have tried to make something on the stove, would she? Tea maybe? She likes lemon tea.

I can't believe I let myself fall asleep.

Bea stamps her foot like she's trying to shake the ash off. "An ounce of prevention is worth a pound of cure. If somebody'd kept an eye on her tonight, we wouldn't have spent half the night shuttling water buckets."

"Ma'am," I say as she turns and walks away, her steps clipped and dangerous.

"I'll tell you what!" Bea shouts over her shoulder. "Somebody better watch her. Or we all ought to sleep with our shoes on. She could set the place on fire all over again, yes she could."

"She doesn't like to sleep with her shoes on. I like to. It's fun," Janet offers.

"One hundred and sixteen windows," Natalie says, rocking back and forth, her eyes down at her shoes. "One hundred and sixteen windows in the front."

"No funny business," I whisper.

"What? What's she saying?" Bea demands, circling back to Natalie.

"How many windows there are in 64 building," I explain.

"What's that got to do with the price of peaches? See, that's what I'm saying. She's unpredictable. And in an emergency—" Bea drills in.

"You know, Mrs. Trixle, ma'am," Donny says, "seems pretty important to me. I sure would want to know how many windows if 64 building was burning down."

Bea's face blanches. "Well," she tut-tuts, "you keep an eye on her, you hear. I won't have my family burned alive because of a retarded girl."

"She's not retarded." My voice cracks.

"Well, she isn't normal, that's for sure."

I rise up inside myself. "You're dead wrong, ma'am. She's better than normal. You just can't see it, that's all."

5. On My Watch

Sunday, January 19, 1936

Nat curls up on the floor in Theresa and Jimmy's room and falls asleep before Mrs. Mattaman has the milk poured and the cookies on a plate. After everything that happened tonight, I'm so keyed up I may never close my eyes again.

Jimmy and I have made beds in the living room with pillows and blankets. We can't stop going over everything we saw tonight. I can almost pretend it didn't happen to my apartment but someone else's instead. It's easier to imagine that, than picture how I will tell my parents.

"But how did it start? Fires don't start on their own," I tell Jimmy.

"Either it was arson or an accident."

"Arson?"

"Could be. Who knows?" Jimmy says.

"But if it was arson, who could have done it? The cons were on lockdown."

"Okay, you two." Mrs. Mattaman comes by and sits on the arm of the couch. "We aren't going to figure it all out tonight. Don't you have something else to talk about? Stamp collecting maybe."

I don't want to talk about stamp collecting.

"I do have a new hobby," Jimmy tells me when she's gone.

"Besides the cockroaches?" I ask. Jimmy used to raise flies but now he's moved on to cockroaches. I don't get the fascination with weird bugs.

"Belly button mold," he whispers.

This is the thing about Jimmy . . . he might actually be serious. "C'mon, mold doesn't really grow in there, does it?"

Jimmy nods firmly. "Yes it does."

"So . . . you're making cheese in your belly button?"

"Belly button cheese," Jimmy confirms with a straight face. "Turns out you can grow anything you want in there."

"Yeah . . . show me the cheese. *This* I have to see."

Jimmy shakes his head. "Not ready yet."

"So what are your plans?" I ask. "Mac and belly button cheese? Parmesan belly button cheese? Or maybe blue belly button cheese—which is extra-stinky?"

Jimmy has his head on his elbows, his pillow facing mine. A smirk spreads over his face. "I'm not sure yet. If you've got ideas, you should tell me."

"Won't it overflow?" I ask.

"You got to harvest," he explains.

"So anybody can start their own cheese factory?"

"It's a competitive business," Jimmy says.

"The bigger the belly button, the better the harvest?"

We're both cracking up now. The idea of Jimmy farming his belly button is too much. I could actually see him do it. That's the funniest part.

Of course, that's when my parents burst in the door still dressed in their evening clothes, my mom clutching her shiny green handbag.

"He's laughing," my mother snaps. "Apparently he's fine."

"Moose." My father's voice is uncharacteristically sharp. "Where's Natalie?"

"She's fine. She's in Theresa's room," I say as Mrs. Mattaman comes out of the kitchen.

"They're just slaphappy, Helen. I told them to talk about something besides the fire. They were so wound up. But you'd have been proud of your Moose, I'll tell you that. He kept his head and got Natalie out of there."

Mr. Mattaman comes out of the bedroom in his undershirt.

"Riv, Anna Maria." My dad steps forward. "'Preciate you helping out like this."

"Of course, Cam, you'd of done the same for us," Mr. Mattaman's deep voice resonates.

"Go on. Go see your girl." Mrs. Mattaman puts her arm around my mother and gives her a squeeze.

My parents head for Theresa and Jimmy's room, then stand watching her from the doorway.

"You talk to Darby?" Riv asks when my dad comes back.

My father shakes his head. Mr. and Mrs. Mattaman exchange a worried look.

"Okay with you if I steal Moose for a minute?" my father asks Jimmy as my mom slips off her high heels and sinks into the Mattamans' sofa.

"Sure, Mr. Flanagan," Jimmy chirps.

"Helen, you go on now. Probably best if I talk to Moose on my own. I'll be up in a few minutes."

"You need me?" Riv asks my dad.

"No thanks, Riv," my dad says.

"I'm gonna stay with the kids, then. Anna Maria wants to

check in on Betty Bomini. She's pretty upset Annie went with Bo instead of her. You know how Betty is with the fainting. But then I guess Annie got to the hospital and they wouldn't let her in. Got to be sixteen."

"Where is Annie now?" I ask.

"She's at Bo's brother's house. She called in and Mrs. Caconi talked to her. She's fine. That Annie's got a good head on her shoulders," Riv tells me, then turns to my dad. "You and Helen are welcome to stay with us, you know that."

"The warden found us a spot. Gonna bunk up at the Chudley house, but you got the better part of the family, that's for sure," my father says.

Mrs. Mattaman smiles. "No doubt there."

"Warden Williams is back, then?" Riv asks.

My father nods.

"Piper was scared to death, poor thing," Mrs. Mattaman reports. "She was watching little Walty all by herself in this hullabaloo. She's not used to babysitting the way your Moose and my Jimmy are."

"Scared everybody, I imagine," my father tells her.

I follow my dad outside, but the cold, damp night air makes me want to return to the Mattamans', where it's warm and cozy and everything is like it always has been. We look at the blackened front of #2E, though neither of us walks over there.

"I hope Mr. Bomini's hand is okay."

"It can't be good if Ollie couldn't get him patched up here," Dad says, his eyes liquid with worry. "Tell me what happened, Moose."

My dad chews his toothpicks as I explain how Theresa and Annie were there and then the fire started and I got Natalie and her button box out, even though she didn't want to go.

I stick with the stuff I feel confident about and skim over the part where I messed up. I'm trying hard to convince myself I didn't fall asleep. That I'm not really to blame.

"Sounds like you did a hero's job getting Nat out like that," Dad says.

I can't look him in the eye. I focus on the dirty watermarks on the balcony floor and then out at the water, black as olives with the same shiny skin. I know he's going to ask me why I didn't notice the fire until it got out of control.

"We done here, Dad? Could I go back to the Mattamans'?"

"I still don't understand what happened," my father says.

I stare at the Mattamans' door, imagining myself buried in the blankets on the living room floor. "I don't want to keep the Mattamans up," I say.

My father puts his hand on my shoulder. "All right, son," he says. "Suppose it can wait till tomorrow."

I duck out from under his hand.

I know he's looking at me. I can feel the heat of his gaze as I pull open the Mattamans' door and disappear inside.

6. Fits and Whispers

Monday, January 20, 1936

When I wake up, it's past ten in the morning, the light is streaming in through the windows, and Mrs. Mattaman is frying sausages. Rocky is setting up his blocks and knocking them down. "Boomy-boomy-boomy," Rocky says. Nat and Theresa are playing the name-that-state game. Theresa points to one of the forty-eight states and Nat tells what page of the book the state is on.

If only this was a regular sleepover and we could just walk home now.

"Natalie," I say, "the fire last night . . . do you know how it started?"

"It started in the kitchen, I think," Natalie says.

"That's what I think. Hey, wait a minute, that's what I said."

"Moose said," Natalie agrees.

"Okay, but what do *you* think?"

Natalie sits on her hands and rocks back and forth. Sometimes dealing with Nat is like playing baseball without the ball. You got to make up the whole game yourself.

"Moose," Mrs. Mattaman calls from the kitchen. "You and Natalie want some breakfast?"

"Sure, Mrs. Mattaman, thanks."

Nat jumps up. Like me, she can always eat, especially when Mrs. Mattaman is doing the cooking.

I head for the kitchen, but Nat gets stuck at the light switch, on-off-on-off.

"Okay, Nat, that's enough," I say, and to my surprise she stops.

"I made you chocolate chip pancakes and sausages, and we've got leftover cinnamon apples," Mrs. Mattaman says.

"Thanks," I tell her.

"She loves cooking for you," Jimmy whispers. "Probably because you'd eat the phone book and say it was delicious. Then burp a few names or a number here and there."

I nod. "Phone book burps are so satisfying."

"Janet Trixle is a big fat liar," Theresa blurts out at the table as she picks the chocolate chips from her pancakes and piles them on her plate.

"Theresa," Mrs. Mattaman scolds. "If you can't say something nice, don't say anything at all."

"What if Janet is a liar? What if she really is? She said Natalie burned down your apartment. But I told her that was a lie and then her mom said it was time for me to go."

Mrs. Mattaman's lips pinch up tight. "Let's not talk about this right now, Theresa."

"She said her daddy is going to be the warden too." Theresa is unstoppable.

"I said not now, Theresa."

"You said not to talk about the fire. I'm talking about her daddy. That's different."

"Let's not talk about the Trixles or the fire," Mrs. Mattaman suggests.

Theresa holds up a pancake that looks like it's full of bullet holes where she picked the chocolate chips out.

"Don't play with your food," Mrs. Mattaman tells her.

We've just finished when my father raps *dum-de-de-dum* on the door. My mother teaches music, but it's my father who likes to sing and dance. "Hey all, good morning," he calls.

"Come on in, Cam," Mrs. Mattaman says. "Can I fix you some breakfast?"

"Nope, I've eaten, thanks. Came to collect my kids, Anna Maria. I appreciate you and Riv pinch-hitting."

"Sure thing, Cam," Mrs. Mattaman says, but her eyes aren't smiling. "Can I have a quick word with you before you go?"

"Of course," my dad answers. "Moose, you go on and help Natalie get everything gathered up."

There's nothing to gather up. This is my father's way of getting rid of me. I march Nat to Theresa's room, then double back to stand behind the sewing machine in the hall.

Mrs. Mattaman takes a deep breath. "There's going to be trouble, Cam," she says in a husky whisper. "Bea and Darby are pitching a fit. They're trying to pin things on Natalie. Bea's all set to call Nat's school. Tell them she starts fires. I'm hoping they'll calm down, but I wouldn't bet on it."

"Why's she so sure it's Natalie?"

"You know they've never liked her. Now they got their teeth into something here and they aren't letting go."

"Anything else I should know?"

"Nothing you can't figure out yourself," Mrs. Mattaman says.

My father groans. "I hate to think Darby would use something like this."

"We'd all hate to think it," Mrs. Mattaman says.

"Okay, Anna Maria. I hear you."

"You know we're behind you one hundred and fifty percent." Mrs. Mattaman again.

"Thanks, Anna Maria. Can't think what we'd do without you two."

Whenever adults get to thanking each other, you know the conversation is over. I scoot back into Theresa's room to get Natalie.

"You hear anything good?" Jimmy asks.

"I was just, you know, inspecting your sewing machine," I say.

"I'm sure," Jimmy says. "Planning on using it real soon. Gonna sew yourself a little skirt?"

"Yep. Gonna have a built-in petticoat too."

"Nice," Jimmy says. He waits, though. He wants the real stuff.

"Your mom thinks the Trixles are on the warpath."

Jimmy nods.

"Jim?" I ask.

"Yeah?"

"I don't want to talk to my dad," I whisper.

He doesn't ask why. Maybe he already knows. You never can tell with Jimmy. "I can come with you, if you want," he says.

"Thanks," I say.

"Sure," he says as we head for the front room.

Out the window, a sailboat rips across the bay with a big tan guy holding the tiller. The lives of people like that seem so easy. My life is never like that.

7. Under the Caconis' Apartment

Monday, January 20, 1936

After the fire last night, all the moms decide we can take a day off from school. This is pretty unusual. It's not worth getting your place burned down for a one-day vacation, but still. Lots of afternoons Jimmy has to work for Bea Trixle at the canteen, but since today is an unexpected holiday, Jimmy isn't on the schedule.

When Jimmy and I get to the Chudley place, we're surprised how large it is. You could play a game of badminton in the living room.

The house is empty—our footsteps echo on the hardwood floors. In one of the bedrooms I see two cots with blankets and pillows. My parents must have slept there. The view is incredible from all the windows though; it's like you can see half of California from up here.

I'm sticking to Jimmy like he's my second skin. That way I know my dad won't ask me any hard questions. It's when Jimmy and I are out on the back porch that the answer to my problem pops into my head. If I find out who or what started the fire, then no one will care if I fell asleep or not.

"Jimmy," I ask, "if you were to solve a mystery, how would you do it?"

"I'd get help. I'd put a team together." Jimmy fiddles with a railing support that has come loose.

"What kind of a team?"

"Annie because she's logical and a good problem solver. Piper—she has access to more information than the rest of us. And me because I understand the science behind fire."

"You've been waiting for me to ask this, haven't you?"

He smiles.

"What about Theresa?" I ask.

"Now that she's Piper's slave, she goes wherever Piper goes. Two for the price of one."

"We should have a meeting, then. Figure this out."

Jimmy nods. "In the secret passageway," he says.

The secret passageway is a crawlspace in 64 building that runs under apartment #1D, an empty apartment, and #1E, Mrs. Caconi's place. We aren't supposed to go down there, but it's pretty easy to get in. We unscrew the screws from the crawl-space door and open it hinge side first. The lock stays locked the whole time.

"Let's go, then," I say.

"What about Natalie?" he asks. "She knows more than any of us."

I cross my arms. "No she doesn't."

Jimmy bites his bottom lip thinking about this. "She was there. She could know something you don't. We should bring her," he concludes.

"I'll see if she'll come. Let's get going now, before my parents think of something else for us to do."

"I'll get Piper and Annie." Jimmy heads for Piper's.

"Mom, I'm taking Natalie," I call up the stairs.

"Did you talk to your father?" my mother asks.

"Uh-huh," I mumble. I did talk to him—not about what he wanted to talk about, but still.

Mom's headed downstairs now like she's on a mission. "Where are you going with Natalie?" she asks.

"To 64."

My mother nods, her eyes watchful.

She has to know I fell asleep. I'm expecting her to bawl me out. "We need to understand how the fire started." I breeze by her, hoping to head her off.

"Do we?" she asks.

I look at her like her brains have seeped out of her ears onto the floor. "Of course," I say.

"There are lots of things that can start a fire. Bad wiring. Damaged lamps. Pennies in the fuse box," my mother says. "64 building is old."

I stare at my mom stupidly. "But Mom, we have to know."

She looks away. "No need to go looking for trouble. It was an accident, Moose. It will all blow over soon enough."

Why wouldn't my mother want to know the truth? Didn't my dad tell her what Mrs. Mattaman said? If Bea calls Nat's school, she could get kicked out.

I look back at Natalie, who is still wearing yesterday's clothes, although her hair is freshly combed and her face is clean.

"Better to leave well enough alone," my mom says.

"Why?" I ask.

"We don't want to find out information we can't handle."

I start to sweat. "Natalie didn't have anything to do with this, Mom."

"Course not," she mumbles, her eyes focused on her hands.

"Natalie," I ask, "do you know how the fire started last night?"

Nat digs at her collarbone with her chin. "Number 2E, number 2E, number 2E."

"Leave her alone, Moose. She doesn't know," my mother says as Theresa knocks, then opens the door with Piper on her heels.

"Come on, Nat." Theresa makes quick circles with her hand. "We need you."

"Where *c'mon Nat*?" she mutters.

"64 building," I say.

"Number 2E?" Nat asks.

"Not exactly," I say, but Nat is already putting buttons back in her button box one by one. She leaves it on the table and trots out after Theresa as if that's where she wanted to go all along.

Theresa is magic sometimes.

My mother is still staring at us, not moving a muscle, barely even breathing . . . but she doesn't stop me.

When we get down to the area under the grates behind 64 building, which we call Chinatown, Jimmy already has the hinges of the secret passageway door off. He and Annie are waiting for us to scoot inside.

"Nice sweater," Annie tells Piper as she hops into the opening. "Is it new?"

"Yep," Piper says. "You want one?"

"Your mom's not going to buy a sweater for me."

"Why not?" Piper asks.

"Piper has loads of money," Theresa informs Annie. "She can buy anything she wants."

"Is that so, Piper?" Annie asks.

"Not hardly," Piper says.

Theresa nods behind her back.

We haven't been down here for a while. I forgot how wet and mildewy it is. Jimmy sneezes as we crawl on our hands and knees through the cobwebs to the part of the passageway directly under the Caconis' place.

One of our secret passageway rules is only whispering is allowed. That way we can hear what goes on in Mrs. Caconi's apartment, but she can't hear us. Today it sounds like Donny Caconi is talking on the phone outside the Caconi apartment.

"Can anybody hear what he's saying?" Jimmy asks.

"That's not nice. It's Donny Caconi. He's our friend," Theresa says.

Piper shrugs. "Sounds like maybe he owes somebody money," she says.

"He tried to borrow from my dad. He said he had a cash problem at his business," Annie says.

"What kind of a business does he have?" I ask.

"Trucking," Annie says.

"I heard that too," Theresa says. "Your dad said: *Sorry buddy, we're barely scraping by ourselves.*"

"Annie, how's your dad's hand, anyway?" I ask.

"He says it doesn't hurt much now."

"No chitchat. We have to get started," Piper announces as if she's the one who called the meeting. We always let her take charge, otherwise she storms off in a huff. "The first thing we got to do is find out what Natalie knows."

"I've asked her a bunch of times. I don't think she knows anything," I say.

"Have you searched your apartment?" Piper asks.

"No," I say.

"Why not?" Piper demands.

"You're right. That should be the first step," Jimmy agrees.

"Of course I'm right. Then we need to ask the cons," Piper declares.

"Why would we ask the cons?" Annie asks.

"Could be hazing," Piper suggests.

"What's that?" Theresa asks.

"It's where people in a club are mean to new members," Annie says.

"You think a con did this?" I ask.

"Of course," Piper says.

"I still don't get it." Theresa's bottom lip sticks out.

"It could be someone's harassing Moose's dad because he's a new warden," Annie explains.

"Cons couldn't set fire to our apartment after they're locked in for the night," I say.

"Who knows?" Piper answers.

"But what's the point of asking them? Why would a con admit what he did?" I ask.

"They like to brag. Otherwise, how will they get credit?" Piper answers.

"But wouldn't it get them in trouble?" I ask.

"They'd say *if* they did it . . . not *who* did it," Jimmy offers.

"They're locked up," Annie insists, sitting back on her heels. "It's not possible."

"They have connections," Piper explains. "They get things done in their own way. Why do you think Chudley got fired?"

"He was helping the cons?" Jimmy asks. "I thought he was just incompetent."

"He was both," Piper says.

"Bad combination," Jimmy says.

"How would we ask the cons? Put a note in our laundry?" Annie asks.

Theresa raises her hand, whips it left, then right. "I know."

"Theresa," Piper calls on her.

"Jimmy's cockroach messengers."

Jimmy smiles like he just got his crystal set working. "I've got a few cockroaches I'm working with. You know how the cons trade cigarettes like money at night? After lockdown, they use cockroaches to get a cigarette from one cell to the next."

"That couldn't be true or I'd know about it," Piper says.

"It is true." Jimmy smiles, his eyes bright. "My dad saw with his own eyes. They tie the cigarettes on their backs with thread and then the con who is supposed to get the delivery, he puts out a chunk of bread on the floor and the cockroach goes to it. Then he unties the cigarette from the cockroach's back."

"So you're going to tie a message to a cockroach's back?" I ask.

"Yep."

"How will you get your cockroach inside the cell house and then out again?" Piper wants to know.

"Can't," Jimmy agrees.

"What's your plan, then?" Annie whacks a cobweb away from her arm.

"The dock," Piper says.

Jimmy nods. He's sitting cross-legged, fiddling with the screwdriver he used to get us in the secret passageway. "Yeah, that's what I was thinking."

"First, let's go to the Flanagans' apartment and look around.

Then we can meet back here to discuss what we find," Piper says.

"Won't we get in trouble? Moose's apartment could be dangerous," Annie says.

"Why? The fire's already out," Theresa says.

"Yeah, but you might fall through the floor where it's burned." Annie again.

"Ohhhh," Theresa says.

"Has anyone said not to go in there?" Piper asks as she crawls toward the Chinatown door.

"No," I say.

"Better to ask forgiveness than permission. That's what my uncle always says." Piper waits for us to catch up.

"Ouch!" Annie bumps her head on the ceiling. "Have you ever asked either?"

"Never needed to," Piper says. "It's all about loyalty anyway. You take care of people and they're loyal to you. Then it doesn't matter if you have permission or not."

"That's the Al Capone model," I say.

"More or less," Piper says.

"Wait." Annie sits back, blocking my way. "We can't all march in there at once. The dock tower guard will notice that for sure."

"Let's go in teams," I suggest.

"Moose and I have to be first," Piper says.

"I'm next." Theresa waves her arm in the air. "I have to be, in case you need something, right, Piper? Right? Natalie, you come with me."

For a second I worry about this. "What if Theresa can't get Nat out of here?" I whisper to Annie.

"Then I'll run get you," Annie says.

"Annie and Jimmy, you're last," Piper commands. "That way Jimmy can close up the passage door."

"Just remember . . . don't mess with anything. This is a crime scene," Jimmy says.

"We don't know it's a crime. It could have been an accident," Annie points out.

"Don't be a spoilsport," Piper tells her.

"Piper, come on. This is Moose's family we're talking about, not some fun game you just thought of." Annie's face is flushed. She flashes a quick look at me.

Piper shrugs. "Let's go, Moose," she orders. "Jimmy, you have a watch. You time us. Wait five minutes between teams."

I follow Piper out with Jimmy's phrase stuck in my head: crime scene. I'm having a hard time accepting that. I don't want this to be about me and whether or not I fell asleep. But I don't want there to be somebody out there targeting us, either. That is just too scary.

8. THE HOUSE OF STICKS

Monday, January 20, 1936

The windows of #2E are shattered. The door is black as the night ocean. The air is thick with the smell of smoke. The door is jammed, the knob is gone.

Piper stands back while I kick it in. I don't have to kick hard before it crumbles, like the house made of sticks in the story of the Three Little Pigs.

"Watch where you put your feet. It's hard to know how stable the floor is," I tell Piper as I take a cautious step through the rubble. Around the living room some things are burned to a crisp, others are ruined by water. Water puddles on the floor, pools in the sagging seat of the chair, and fills the light fixture like a fish bowl.

Natalie's room is mostly okay, but mine is scorched, the closet a mess of ashes on the floor.

I stare at everything, trying to take it all in. Did someone do this to us?

It couldn't have been Natalie. I wasn't asleep for that long . . . . was I? But if not Natalie, who? Can your house get burned down by accident? My mouth is dry. My head begins to throb like someone is digging my brain out with a trowel.

"Hey Piper," I say, "why aren't there officers here? Don't they want to know how this started?"

"Adults don't make sense," she says. "Everybody knows that."

I'm too upset to find this funny. This is my house. Doesn't anyone care it burned down?

"You think it started in the kitchen?" Piper asks as Natalie and Theresa come in the broken front door and make a path through the living room.

The place is probably safe. The flooring seems sound. The only really dangerous part is the broken glass and breathing in the ash. I know my parents wouldn't like Natalie in here, but right now the only thing that matters is figuring this out.

"Give everyone a job," Piper whispers to me, "and you'll earn their loyalty."

I roll my eyes. This isn't about loyalty. This is about Piper ordering people around, but I do what she says anyway. I don't want a showdown with Piper.

"Okay," I say, "Piper, you're in the—"

"Not me!" She points at Nat and Theresa. "Them."

"Theresa, you go with Nat. Help her find what she needs."

Theresa puts her hands on her hips. "That's not helping with the investigation," she declares. "That's busy work."

"No it's not. Natalie may know more than I do about what happened. Something here might jog her memory. Watch where she goes. Watch what she does. She was sleeping on my floor the night of the fire."

Theresa nods solemnly, her eyes the size of plums.

I should be in the kitchen looking for clues, but I want to find my baseball glove, which is probably in Nat's room.

"Hey, Theresa? Nat? Is my baseball glove in there?"

"Wait, um, hey, here it is!" Theresa calls out. She runs out of Nat's room, holding my glove like a sleeping baby.

"Yes!" I slip my fingers inside and close my fist. I am never taking it off.

I run my gloveless hand over the stuff that still looks like my stuff. My pillow, the bedside table, the pennant from the Seals game, my history book. I never thought I'd care about my history book. It's strange what a fire will do to you.

I'm about to look for my report on Roosevelt when Annie comes to the door. She moves slowly toward me, testing the floor before she takes the next step. She stops and looks up at me, her blue eyes full of concern. "This is bad." Then she sees the glove. "Hey." She smiles as big as a baseball field. "You found it!"

I smile back at her. Annie knows there's nothing like your own glove.

"We should check out the rest of the place," she says.

My parents' room is scorched in one stripe from the doorway down one wall, like a black lick of fire came through.

The kitchen is a burned-out hole. Jimmy is on his hands and knees sifting through the ashes. On the floor are a melted fork, a handle-less skillet, the square icebox now black as the devil's cupboard. Piper has her head in the broom closet.

"If it was arson, what are we looking for?" I ask Jimmy.

"I was hoping for something obvious . . . a metal gasoline can, lighter fluid, matches."

In the living room, Annie is trying to piece together bits of fabric from the chair.

At first, I couldn't smell anything but smoke. But now my

nose seems to be deadened to the smoke smell. How much of a smell can you smell, until you can't smell it anymore?

"Maybe we should do a reenactment," Annie suggests.

"Not much to reenact," I say. "Nat was asleep on the floor of my room."

"Why was she sleeping in your room?" Theresa asks.

"She does that when I babysit," I say.

"Maybe she gets scared." Theresa again.

"Maybe," I say.

"Hey," Piper calls from the kitchen. "I found something."

Within seconds we are clustered around Piper, stirring up a new cloud of ashes, which starts Jimmy coughing.

"What?" I ask.

Piper pulls a half-burned hatbox out of the rubble. "Janet Trixle's pixie house."

"What is Janet Trixle's pixie house doing up here?" I ask.

"Do you know anything about this, Theresa?" Piper wants to know.

Theresa and Janet are on-again, off-again friends. Theresa shakes her head. "Nope."

"Maybe Janet was having a pixie campout with pixie marshmallows cooked over the Flanagans' stove," Piper says.

"Did she visit yesterday?" Annie asks me.

"Nope," I say.

"She could have left the stove on." Jimmy clicks his tongue the way he does when he's thinking hard about something. But then I hear footsteps.

Annie's head turns. So does mine.

Piper puts her finger over her mouth as the big-booted footsteps come closer.

"Who's in there?" Darby bellows through his bullhorn.

"Uh-oh," Theresa whispers as Trixle pounds into the living room.

"Who gave you permission to go poking around?"

"I did," I say.

"And who gave *you* permission?" Trixle booms.

"Nobody. It's my place," I tell him.

"Not now it isn't. It ain't safe and I want all of you out. The warden's got a task force assigned. They're the only ones should be in here."

"But . . ." Theresa nods toward the pixie house.

Annie shushes Theresa behind Trixle's back. Darby catches this from the corner of his eye. He turns around. "What's the matter, Theresa?" he asks.

Theresa seals her lips and shakes her head.

"Spit it out," he barks.

"Theresa gets upset when grown-ups yell," Piper covers for her, smooth as butter.

"Mind your own business, Piper. I'm asking Theresa," Darby says.

"What's a task force?" Theresa wants to know.

"It's a team of people assigned to find out something," Annie whispers.

"Like us," Theresa says.

"Not like you," Darby growls. "You are making a nuisance of yourselves. That's all you're doing."

Theresa opens her mouth to tell him off, but Annie puts her hand on Theresa's arm, and Theresa snaps her mouth shut with the words safely inside.

"We'll be done end of day tomorrow. Then Moose can

come get what he needs. But all of the rest of you"—he points in an arc over our heads—"have no business in here, period."

Darby tramps through the ash to the bashed-in front door and waits for us to come out.

Theresa moves her hand in a rapid rotation like Annie should come close. Annie scrunches down so her ear is the same height as Theresa's mouth.

I don't hear all of what Theresa says, but it's something about the pixie house. I think she's asking if she should tell about that. Annie shakes her head.

I get my pillow and leave my history book—I've come to my senses about that. And the homework? Forget about it.

The baseball glove has never left my hand.

Piper takes the half-burned pixie house and drops it inside my pillowcase with my pillow. *Gee, thanks,* I think.

Annie and Jimmy are already outside. Natalie is agitated. She's in her room rocking from one foot to the other.

"Nat," I say, "come on."

"No 'come on,'" she says.

"Trixle doesn't like you. We have to get out of here," I whine.

Why am I telling her this? She won't get it, but to my surprise she moves forward, out of her room and past Trixle, still guarding the door

"Trixle doesn't like you," she says when she walks by him.

Trixle stamps his cigarette out with his foot. He acts like he didn't hear, but I'm pretty sure he did.

9. ANNIE AND ME AT THE SWINGS

Monday, January 20, 1936

"Where should we go? Back down to the secret passageway?" Theresa whispers.

"Not with Trixle watching. How about our house?" Jimmy suggests. "Mom's in the city getting groceries."

"C'mon, Nat. We're going to my house," Theresa says.

"Moose," Piper calls.

But I'm already headed the other direction. I don't feel so great. "I'll be there in a few minutes," I tell her.

"Moose, we're meeting *now,*" Piper commands.

But I keep walking along the balcony away from the Mattamans'. I don't know where I'm going . . . I just want to be alone. What I really want is to go back to my room, but I can't with Trixle standing right there. Nowhere else on the island is mine. I don't have a place anymore.

I head up to the parade grounds and sit on the swing. I'm way too big for a swing, but I don't care. I just sit there. Like always, the parade grounds is full of gulls. I watch as one gull opens his beak, cocks his head back, and cries his mournful cry. Seagulls are big whiners. They are never happy.

I look up from the gulls and there is Annie walking across

the cement, the wind blowing her dress to one side as she battles to keep it down.

Annie parks in the empty swing next to mine. "Hi," she says.

"Hi," I mutter.

"You want to, you know, talk?" she asks as she times the arc of her swing with mine so that we are going forward and backward in the same moment.

I shrug.

"Seeing your place like that must have been hard."

"Yeah," I mumble, looking back toward 64. I don't want to say too much. I'm afraid I might cry. Guys aren't supposed to cry. My dad does once in a while and it really bugs me.

We're both barely swinging at all with our feet pushing off the ground instead of pumping the air. I kick some sand low, covering her shoes with sand. She kicks a load back.

We continue like this, until we have to take off our shoes and pour out the sand. Annie peels off her white socks and turns them inside out. A thump of sand falls out and then a light scattering.

"Annie?"

"Yeah."

"I don't know how the fire started," I whisper.

"I know you don't."

"But Annie?"

"Yeah."

My voice cracks. "I was asleep."

"Just because you were asleep doesn't mean Natalie did it."

"It wasn't Natalie," I snap.

"Sorry, I thought that was what you were worried about."

I lean forward, digging a hole in the sand with my toe. "It is."

Annie nods. "Has she ever used matches or turned the burner on?"

"I've never seen her with matches. She has turned the burner on."

"Would she do that at night?"

I don't answer this, can't answer it. I don't know.

"When you fell asleep, where was she?" Annie asks.

"In my room on the floor."

"And then you woke up and . . ."

"Everything was on fire."

"Look, we'll figure this out, okay? You don't need to do it all by yourself."

"But it was me who fell asleep."

"It was late. I was asleep too."

"But you weren't babysitting."

"Maybe you should talk to your folks about this, Moose."

"NO!" I half shout.

Annie says nothing else. We swing a while. The swing chains make a *vreeek-vrok-vreek-vrok* sound. We aren't swinging so much as kicking back and forth, but they're still noisy.

"We'll make a chart, you know? Figure out all the possibilities. We'll be really organized about it. We'll find out the truth," she whispers. "That's all we can do." She leans forward in her swing, stops her motion with her heel, and looks at me. "That going to be okay?"

I try to smile, but my lips feel like they're anchored to a rock. Still, I appreciate how she's trying to help. There's never been a better friend than Annie.

10. A Bad Day for Pixies

Monday, January 20, 1936

When we get back to the Mattamans', everyone has piled in Jimmy and Theresa's room. I settle on Jimmy's bed. Annie joins Piper and Theresa on Theresa's bed. Piper hogs the pillow, of course. Natalie is standing up by herself so no one will accidentally bump her. She likes it better this way.

"Where have you been?" Piper demands.

"Out on the parade grounds," I say.

"Playing baseball?"

"No," I mumble.

Piper crosses her arms. Her eyes travel from Annie to me and back again.

"C'mon, we're making progress here. Let's keep at it," Jimmy says. "Why would Janet just walk in Moose's kitchen and decide to have a pixie campout? She could have done that at her own house."

"No, she couldn't." Theresa shakes her head. "Her mom doesn't let her turn on the stove."

"But wouldn't the same rules apply at my apartment?" I ask.

"Maybe, maybe not," Jimmy says.

"Shouldn't we tell an adult about Janet's pixie house?" Annie says.

"Why? What do they know?" Piper asks.

"Why? What do they know?" Natalie repeats, dipping her head down, her bottom lip sucked into her mouth.

"Somebody has to talk to Janet," Piper insists.

Theresa waves her hand in thc air. "Mc. I will!"

"Theresa for sure. But who else?" Piper again.

"How about Jimmy?" I suggest.

Theresa shakes her head so hard, her hair whips into her face. "Not Jimmy. Moose. She likes Moose better."

"Yeah, Moose. You're really popular with the seven-year-olds." Jimmy smiles as he winds rubber bands around his finger.

"Gee thanks, but I'm not getting near Bea Trixle without body armor."

"You won't have to see Bea. Theresa will bring Janet up here," Jimmy says.

"But wait . . . what if it *is* Janet?" Theresa asks.

We stare at Theresa.

"If it was Janet, it was an accident. We all know Janet would not intentionally burn Moose's apartment down," Annie tells her.

"That's right," I say.

"Come on, Piper," Annie says. "Let's go to my house. It will be weird if we're waiting in the living room while Theresa and Moose talk to Janet."

When Piper and Annie are gone, Jimmy parks himself in the kitchen and I get Natalie set up in the living room with her favorite Mattaman book: a travel book about the states. Theresa marches up to the Trixles' to get Janet.

Janet has her hair braided in braids so tight, they pull her eyebrows out of place, giving her a permanently surprised look.

She is a bit wacky anyway. For one thing, no one knows if she believes in her imaginary friends—the pixies—or not. The pixies drive her parents crazy, so she has to pretend they aren't real. It isn't totally clear if she believes in them and pretends they aren't real, or doesn't believe in them and pretends they are. Then too, she can get really bossy. Nobody likes that. Still, given who her parents are, she's not half bad.

"Janet." Theresa's face is stern like she's a teacher. Her pencil hovers over a pad of paper waiting for something to write down. "What happened to your old pixie house?"

Janet squints for a minute as if this helps her remember, then shrugs.

"You don't know?" Theresa's dark black eyebrows are furrowed.

Janet shakes her head.

"When was the last time you remember seeing it?" I ask.

"I don't know. My pixies like to travel," Janet explains. "I've taken them everywhere on this island."

"How about Moose's apartment?" Theresa asks.

"We're not supposed to go in there," Janet answers.

"We're talking about before the fire," Theresa says.

Janet looks at Theresa. "We've played there before, you know that."

Theresa blushes, then glances nervously at me.

Janet pulls at one of her braids. "Why are you asking me all these questions?"

"No reason," Theresa chirps.

Janet scowls. "There is so a reason."

"No reason I'm going to tell you," Theresa corrects.

Janet bugs her eyes at Theresa. "You have to tell."

"No I don't," Theresa says.

"Do so."

"Do not."

Janet's hands fly to her hips. "Do you want me to tell my mommy?"

"Go ahead, because we have evidence," Theresa announces. She has written *EVEDENSE* in big letters on her pad.

"Evidence? What kind of evidence?" Janet demands.

Oh great. I should have known this would get out of hand. "Theresa, calm down."

Theresa nods obediently. "Never mind about that," she says.

Janet frowns. Her lips are large and rubbery like a grown man's lips on a seven-year-old girl's face. When she frowns, they take over. "I know . . . you want *me* to have set that fire instead of Natalie."

"Nat didn't start the fire," Theresa says.

"Did so."

"Did not."

"Did so. Mommy said."

"She doesn't know everything," Theresa says.

"She knows more than you do," Janet says.

"All right, let's drop this, okay? We found your pixie house burned in our kitchen. That's all."

"It's okay," Janet says. "The pixies weren't in it."

"But what was it doing there?" Theresa asks.

"Hey wait a minute . . . . if it was burned, how did you know what it was?" Janet demands.

"It was only partway burned," I explain.

"I'm not allowed to use matches and neither are the pixies," Janet says.

"You have, though. I've seen you," Theresa announces.

"I tried that once but they bended, remember?" Janet again.

"Were you in our kitchen when you tried?" I ask.

"No!" both Janet and Theresa say.

"Okay, we were just asking. We don't think you did it," I say.

"Yes we do," Theresa says.

Janet jumps off the bed. "I want my pixie house back!"

Theresa shakes her head in a hard wide-swinging no. "It's evidence."

"I'm going to tell my dad, then. He'll fix your wagon."

"What's that mean?" Theresa asks.

"It means you're going to get paddled."

"I am not!"

"Theresa, give her back the pixie house," I tell her.

Theresa's lip sticks out. Her face gets all squinched up. She stomps into her closet and comes out with the burned hatbox. Only one side of it is left. You can still see a circus lion and the black-and-white bars Janet drew. Janet's pixies are always either in jail or in the circus.

"This is a bad day for pixie people," Janet whispers. She walks out, but then she comes back. "Don't talk to my parents about the pixies. They don't believe in them," she says.

"Okay," I say.

"But you believe in them?" She stares me down.

"Of course," I say.

She nods solemnly, then heads for the door.

Theresa listens to this, but she doesn't say a word. Her shoulders are in a monumental slump. "We didn't find out anything. There is nothing here." She waves her EVEDENSE pad at me. "What are we going to do now, Moose?"

"Do I have to know everything?"

Theresa nods her head.

"I guess we'll put Jimmy's cockroach messengers to the test."

Theresa sighs. "I've never depended on a cockroach before."

"No," I say, "me neither."

11. The Best Pitching Arm

Tuesday, January 21, 1936

If the first day my dad starts his job, they burn our apartment down, I don't want to consider what's next. Luckily I was so tired last night, I couldn't think about anything.

We slcpt at the Chudleys', and from the ragged way my dad looks this morning, I can tell Natalie didn't sleep. Which means my parents took turns staying up with her, because you never know with Natalie if she'll decide to take a midnight swim in the bay or flush the toilet until it overflows or take a walk and never come back.

"Hey, Dad," I say as my father boosts himself up onto the counter and starts rummaging through the shelves looking for coffee.

"Do you need help with Natalie today?" I'm angling to stay home. I want to figure out how the fire started while the "crime scene" is still fresh.

"Yes, but it's more important that you go to school," he answers. He jumps off the counter, no coffee in hand.

"My homework was due yesterday and now it's gone. That paper I spent so much time on, remember? The one on President Roosevelt."

"Our apartment burned down, Moose. Your teacher will understand."

"What if she makes me do it over again?"

"Then you'll do it over again. If that's the only bad thing that comes of this, we should consider ourselves lucky."

"Are you sure you don't need help with Natalie?" I ask as he slides his arm into his jacket.

"Moose." He rubs his chin, and makes a face like he's surprised to feel whiskers there.

"Okay, okay," I sigh, then grab my glove. May as well head for the dock now. It's early, but I'm ready to leave, and there's usually a few guys playing ball on South field before the first bell rings.

The air is damp and the sky is so packed with fog, you can't even see Angel Island. Only a few patches of blue sky peek through overhead. When I get to the dock, Theresa is hopping down the 64 building stairs, banging her lunch pail against her legs.

"You're taking the early boat?" I ask.

"Piper needs her messenger." She nods toward Piper, who is just coming through the sally port.

"Why are you on the early boat?" I ask when she's in hearing range.

"Leadership," she answers with a smug smile.

"Leadership, huh? You teaching them the Al Capone model for influencing people?"

"Very funny."

"No really . . . maybe you could write a book."

"Donny!" Theresa says the name like it's everybody's favorite song.

"Hey Moose." He tips his hat at me as the foghorn booms so loud, you can feel the vibrations in your feet. "How are you doing this morning, buddy?"

"Okay," I say.

He nods. "Early for school, isn't it?"

"I'm gonna play a little ball before the bell," I say.

"I heard you play first base." Donny speaks just to me.

How did he know?

"So are you good?" he asks.

The blood rises to my face. "I'm decent."

He nods like he's a judge deciding on this, then smiles, his dimples deepening. "Thought you might be able to give me a few pointers."

Donny Caconi wants pointers from me. I know he's trying to pump me up after my place burned down and everything, but still.

"Sure," I say.

He and Piper and Theresa are all watching me now.

Donny puts his hand in his pants pocket, then takes it out again. When his fingers open, I'm expecting something dazzling and miraculous, but all he has are bottle caps.

He jingles them in his hand. "Think you could throw one of these puppies past that barrel?" He points at a red drum barrel halfway across the dock.

"Course, but could we use a baseball?" I'm itching to show him how well I throw. Nobody can throw a bottle cap as well as a baseball.

"You have one?" he asks.

"Sure. Oh. No. All I have is my glove."

"Baseball in your old place?"

I nod.

"Too bad, buddy. For now let's just use these." He jingles the bottle caps again. "They'll do in a pinch. Okay with you?" He waits for my nod.

The drum isn't that far away. I don't see how either of us could miss. "I got two bucks says I can throw one of these puppies past the barrel from right here." His shiny toe taps the ground.

"Two bucks?" I mumble. Who has that kind of money?

"How much, then?" he asks.

My face heats up. "Um, uhhh."

Piper moves in. She's dressed in her best Leadership clothes. A white blouse and dark bow that matches her skirt. "I can chip in."

"Me too! I have money! Me!" Theresa raises her arm and swings it wildly. She hands Donny a dime.

"Will you look at that." Donny includes everyone in his dimpled smile. "You got fans."

I wiggle my hand in my pocket and find the nickel I've had there since Piper first told me she needed flowers.

"Come on, Moose, don't be a chicken." Piper gives Donny a dollar. A dollar? That's a lot, even for her.

"I guess your girlfriend here thinks you can do it." Donny nods toward Piper.

Piper's cheeks get pink as cotton candy. "I'm not his girlfriend," she mutters.

Donny laughs. "She's not your girlfriend," he whispers to me, eyeing her all the while.

"I only have a nickel," I say.

"No problem, we'll work with what you got. I'll match

your bet." Donny raises his hands in surrender. "Got two bucks, thirty cents says you can get this cap past the barrel and I can't."

"What if we both make it?" I ask.

"You'll get the whole kitty: two bucks, thirty cents."

"So wait. I get all the money if we both get it past? That doesn't seem fair."

Donny nods. "Be worth it to see how you do things. Your arm in action. Be an education."

Theresa frowns. "Moose could show you without a bet."

"Sure," I say, the pressure in my chest easing.

Donny shakes his head. "You should be paid for your time. Make it worth your while," he tells me like he's my coach.

"Hey, thanks," I say, standing up a little straighter. He's probably just doing this on account of he feels bad for me, but I like it anyway.

"It's not that far," Piper adds, eyeing the drum. "Even I could make it."

"I don't think so, boss," Theresa tells her.

Donny nods to Piper, talking to her as if she's somebody too. "You want to bet on Moose or on yourself?"

"Moose," Theresa answers for her.

Donny's eyes don't leave Piper's face. "I asked Piper."

"Moose," Piper says.

"Looks like she's your girlfriend to me," Donny whispers. "All right then." He takes a small piece of white chalk out of his pocket and marks an X on the dock boards. "You go first."

Donny sinks back on his heels. "Call me a fool. I mean, you guys play all the time, but I'm gonna give it a shot." He smiles. "You first, Moose. Got to see what I'm up against."

I put my feet on the X, take a bottle cap from his cool palm, and pitch it hard and fast in a direct line. It hits the wood, bounces once, then stops next to the drum. Not a bad throw. Not bad at all.

"Made it," I say.

"Nice," Donny says. "But it didn't go past."

"It's even with it. Not past it," Theresa agrees.

My stomach sinks. First I fall asleep when I'm supposed to be babysitting, then I can't execute a simple throw. What's the matter with me? A warden's kid is supposed to be better than this. Still, if I can't do it, I doubt Donny will be able to either.

Donny takes his hat off, smoothes his hair back. "Might as well face the music here." He fingers the bottle cap.

Donny looks carefully at the drum, winds up, but doesn't let go, winds up again and lets it fly. I'm pretty sure from the way his arm moves, I've got him beat, but the bottle cap cuts through the air like a skipping stone. It arcs higher than mine and lands a good five feet farther. Clearly beyond the drum.

"Would you look at that? You really are a good teacher! Then again, probably just dumb luck," Donny says. "What say we try again? Double or nothing."

I shake my head a firm no.

"You sure?" Donny asks. "You almost had me. I got lucky is all. Bottle caps threw you off your game. Takes a time or two to get used to them is all. We'll try your baseball next time." He shoves his hand in his pocket and jingles the change in there. "I'm not going to keep your money. We'll chalk it up to practice."

“It’s only fair. We had a bet. Moose *lost,*” Piper says.

I wish she would keep her mouth shut. Maybe she’s got money to burn, but the rest of us don’t.

“He’s going to be a man about it too. Honor his bets. Moose is a stand-up guy.” Donny smiles at me.

“Don’t you want some more tips from him?” Theresa asks.

“Sure thing.” Donny pulls the brim of his hat down low. “But we got to get on the boat here, missy,” he says.

We all look out to where the bow of the *Coxe* is cutting through the fog toward us.

This was all just a distraction to make me feel better and we both know it. He’ll return our money. Course he will. But when the ferry puts down the gangplank, he gets on without looking back.

12. Just Plain Mean

Tuesday, January 21, 1936

By the time I get to school, Piper has told every last person about the fire. The trouble is, nobody believes it was an accident. Every kid is sure it was Al Capone who burned our place down. We didn't do what he said. We didn't treat him right. We didn't buy him cigars or silk underwear or cannolis and he got mad.

The rumors are out of hand. By the end of the day, Piper has everyone believing the fire consumed all of Alcatraz, and the prisoners are on a boat floating in the bay—waiting to attack the city.

Even Mrs. Twiggs is impressed. But when I tell her what really happened, she lets me know how sorry she is, then tells me I will need to redo my paper and turn it in next week. Piper, on the other hand, gets a free ride and her house was nowhere near the fire. "Every student is different. Some are more fragile than others. Piper is quite sensitive," Mrs. Twiggs explains when I take it up with her.

Piper . . . sensitive? I think I'm going to be sick.

On the ferry home, I tell Jimmy all about what happened with school and then about Donny and the bottle caps.

"So he outthrew you?" Jimmy asks.

"Pretty much," I say.

"With bottle caps?"

"I wanted to use a ball, but I didn't have one."

"And he kept the money?"

I look out at the water, green as seaweed today. "I'm sure he'll give it back next time we see him. He's not going to take money from us."

Jimmy nods uncertainly. "I've seen you throw a million times. I can't imagine he can throw better than you can."

It's true. Donny's throw wasn't that great, but I'm not going to say this out loud. Even to Jimmy. It makes me sound like I'm full of myself.

Instead, I change the subject. "When are we going to try the cockroaches?" I ask.

"I got Saturday off. We can do it then." Jimmy works really hard. He doesn't get money, either, just credit for the Mattamans' groceries. Even so, the Mattamans seem to have less money than anyone else.

I'm not wild about waiting until Saturday, and I'm concerned about pinning all of my hopes on a few scummy bugs. "Could you get a day off before then?"

"Did you forget who I work for?" he asks.

I can't even imagine having Bea Trixle for a boss. She's almost as bad as Darby. Bea and Darby Trixle deserve each other.

Once the boat docks, I say goodbye to Jimmy and head up the switchback. I'd like to work a bit more on the Janet angle. I know Janet is a good kid, she would never have started a fire on purpose; but it could have happened accidentally.

It won't be so easy to run into Janet now, though. I'm not going to knock on her door and risk coming face-to-face with

Bea or Darby. When we lived in 64 building, I saw Janet more, but now that we're parked at the Chudleys' I probably won't.

I don't like living at the Chudley house. When I want to play ball, I have to walk all the way down to 64 to get Annie, then back up to the parade grounds to play. Plus, it's lonely up there. We have the same mournful gulls, the same lonely foghorn, but it all seems creepier when you're catawampus to the cell house.

My father says the task force is still inspecting #2E. He says it will be at least two weeks until we can move back even with the crew of convict carpenters working overtime. I don't like to think about felons pawing through my stuff, but I'll deal with it if that's how we'll get back home.

The big question is will Nat ever be able to sleep up here. With no sleep, she gets touchy—almost explosive, and everybody treats her like she's made of cut paper. Then my parents start dragging around like they haven't slept since last Thanksgiving.

It doesn't help that we don't have our stuff at the Chudleys'. Our whole kitchen was lost in the fire. Any time we need something, it'll mean another trip down to 64 building to borrow pans, spatulas, colanders, and serving spoons. And guess who's going to make all those trips.

Yours truly, pack animal.

Before I even walk in the door, my mother hands me a grocery list: salt, sugar, tea, spaghetti, and tomato sauce. I've managed to steer clear of Bea since Sunday night. But when I get down to the canteen, there she is, shelving soup cans.

I stall, peering in the window, wishing Jimmy would

show up. I'm ready to hunt him down, when Annie and her mom arrive.

"What are you doing?" Annie asks me as her mom opens the canteen door, the bell tinkling her arrival.

"I have to get stuff for supper."

Annie looks through the window at Bea Trixle, then back at me. "Want me to?"

I hand her the list. "Thanks," I say.

She pushes open the door. Bea is talking to Mrs. Bomini, but her eyes flash in my direction. "That Flanagan girl burns the place down and nobody does squat."

I should ignore this and wait outside for Annie, but I can't stop myself from going in. "Natalie didn't have anything to do with the fire, Mrs. Trixle, ma'am," I say as politely as a person who wants to slug another person can possibly manage.

"Apparently the fire started by its own self." Bea's voice is thick with sarcasm.

Mrs. Bomini opens her mouth to say something, but I cut her off.

"The task force hasn't released their report."

"I don't need a task force to know what I know," she says, her face red as a rash. "What's more, I don't appreciate you accusing my Janet."

Annie has my arm. She's trying to pull me out the door, but my stubborn feet won't budge. "Moose, c'mon."

My voice shakes with the effort of keeping my temper in check. "It's not fair to blame Natalie."

"Tell you what's not fair," Bea tells Mrs. Bomini. "Being

stuck up there with no fire escape. And your husband burning his hand because of a girl who should be locked up."

"Now, now," Mrs. Bomini says. "That was an accident."

"But it wouldn't have happened if that Flanagan girl hadn't started the blaze. That's my point," Bea says.

"You have no proof it was Natalie," I tell her.

"You have no proof it wasn't. Darby has told me all about it," Bea counters. "We should go to the *newspapers*. That's what we should do, and we ought to call that school of hers. I couldn't live with myself if I thought those poor little children might be in danger because of her."

"Oh for heaven's sake, Bea," Mrs. Bomini says. "Is that really necessary?"

"I'm suggesting what any upstanding citizen ought to do."

"Can't you wait for the report?" I insist.

She snorts. "No one has the guts to blame the associate warden's daughter and that's the truth."

"Ma'am." My chest strains like it might pop.

"Calm down," Annie whispers.

"She's spreading lies," I say.

"*I'm* spreading lies?" Bea is fit to be tied.

"She needs someone to blame," Annie whispers, her mouth pressed tight against my ear. She takes my hand and pulls me out the door. The second we get outside, she drops my hand and shoves her hands in her pockets.

"Natalie's an easy target, that's all. My dad says Bea's scared. 64 doesn't have fire escapes and it should. That's one good thing that's come out of this. They're looking at building some now." Annie's face is flushed. She doesn't look at me directly when she says this.

"Annie, your parents don't think Natalie . . ."

Annie shakes her head. "Nope. Bea's just plain mean. That's all."

"The task force will clear Natalie." I say this like I'm absolutely positive of it. But once the words are out, they seem flimsy, like I could knock them down with my finger.

13. Al Capone Is My English Teacher

Tuesday, January 21, and Wednesday, January 22, 1936

After I say goodbye to Annie, I head over to Doc Ollie's yard. I may have lost my nickel, but Doc Ollie's sister is a big gardener, and she's not stingy about her flowers. She always says a garden is for everyone to enjoy. I pick a daisy and then ring the warden's bell.

Piper's mom answers. "Moose," she says, her eyes on the flower.

"Is Piper here? This is, uh, for her." I blush hot as a radiator.

"Aren't you the sweetest thing. I was wondering where Piper was getting all the presents from. She's at her grandma's, but boy will she be sorry she missed this."

I open my mouth to tell her that I've never given Piper a present in my life, but how do I say that without sounding rude?

"When will she be back?" I ask.

"Tomorrow, but I'll make sure she gets it. Of course I will. Thanks, dear," she says, and then she's gone.

I stand staring at the closed door. Who is Piper's secret admirer anyway? Not that I care or anything. I only kissed her one time. Okay, one and a half, but still.

On the way back to the Chudleys' I start thinking about the task force report. Is there any way to find out what's in it before everyone else? The only person who would know is Piper. Where is she when I need her?

At the Chudleys', the day's dishes sit in the sink. Flies cluster around a honey spill. The bacon is on the counter, congealed grease in the pan. Why didn't Mom take the leftover food back to Doc Ollie's icebox. Isn't that the plan?

She's tired, that's why. Between the fire and Nat staying up all night, she's a wreck.

When she finally gets supper on the table, the spaghetti noodles are watery and the tomato sauce tastes like cough medicine. Natalie is so agitated, she eats standing up. My mother is so tired, she doesn't care.

By bedtime, I have a headache from thinking about the task force and the cockroaches and Natalie and her eye contact trouble and then this sleep problem on top of everything else. Right now she's in her room, rocking from one foot to the other. Every time we persuade her to lie down, she sits bolt upright like she's afraid to fall asleep. Did the fire scare her? Or does she just dislike the Chudleys'? She held it together so well the night of the fire, but now she's a mess.

"The sun come up this morning?" she whispers.

"It's bedtime, Nat," I say. "You have to go to bed first."

"I have to go to bed first," Nat parrots.

"Yes," I say in a rush of hopefulness. At least she hasn't slid back to calling herself Natalie the way she used to. That bugged me. Only insane people and batters on a losing streak talk about themselves in the third person.

I play the Stupid Moose game. I call out wrong answers to simple math problems, pretend to confuse the order of the weekdays and the number of buttons in her box. I balance marshmallows on my nose, flicker the lights for her, offer up my toothbrush, and take her to the parade grounds swings. But nothing helps.

I sleep fitfully until I hear someone knocking on the front door. I head downstairs and peek out the window to see who is knocking. The outside light shines down on the blue uniform of Darby Trixle.

"Everybody okay in there?" he calls.

I open the door a crack. "The lights are blazing all over the house. I thought I better check on you," Darby explains.

"We're fine," I tell him.

He nods. "Bo Bomini said the same thing happened last night. I saw the reports."

The reports go to Warden Williams and to his boss, the head of the Bureau of Prisons. That's the chain of command as my father explained it to me.

Why did I open the door? Knowing Darby, he would have broken it down if I didn't open it.

I hear footsteps on the stairs behind me. Good. My father can handle this.

"Dad, it's Officer Trixle," I say.

My father swings the door open wide. "Can I help you with something, Darby?"

"All the lights been on all night long. I thought you might be needing something, sir."

My father nods. "I'm afraid Natalie is still getting over the trauma of the fire."

"You need help watchin' her? Make sure she don't get in trouble?"

"She's scared," my father tells him. "Not dangerous."

"The missus says she isn't going to her school anymore."

"School holiday this week," my father explains as my mom pads down the stairs in her slippers.

"Darby, hello." She pulls her bathrobe tight around herself. "What's the trouble?"

"Nothing, honey. Go on back to bed."

"Why is Darby here?" she asks.

"Darby was checking on us is all. Just being neighborly."

"I see." My mother gives Darby a smile that would cool molten lava.

"Guess you're all set, then." Darby salutes. "You need something, give a holler."

"Sure thing, Darby, thank you." My father smiles as if he means it.

"Why is it his business whether our lights are on or off?" my mother whispers as soon as the door is shut.

"It isn't unreasonable for him to check on us," my father tells her.

"Don't kid yourself. He's hanging around hoping for a problem."

"Helen, you don't know that."

"Like heck I don't."

"Dad," I say, "Nat's going back to school on Sunday night, right?"

"Of course," my mom says.

"And she'll be able to sleep there, right?" I ask.

"Right," my father says. "We just have to get through this week."

"She asleep now?" my mom asks hopefully.

"Almost," Dad says.

"Ahhh." My mother's voice is flat as a penny. "My turn. Go on, get some sleep."

If only I'd stayed up the night of the fire, maybe none of this would have happened. Could my mistake have caused all this?

In the morning I drag myself out of bed and peek in Nat's room. Natalie is wide awake. My mother is curled up in Nat's bed. How can one sister cause so much trouble?

When Nat's upset, she likes her purple blanket. We didn't find it when we got our stuff, but maybe we just missed it.

Before I even eat breakfast, I head down to #2E. Already the place looks a bit better. The burned-out stove and the icebox are gone. The kitchen cupboards are being rebuilt. The hall closet is cleaned out. The ashes in my room are swept into a neat pile. I sit on the floor and begin sifting the dirt, sawdust, and ashes. I find the spine of my baseball book, a piece of a drawing of a sphinx I did for a project on the Egyptians, the metal end of a pencil, a half-burned slipper, a lamp cord, and the heel of an old sock.

Natalie's room is almost untouched. A lot of her stuff is still in there, but we already brought her everything we thought might comfort her. Trying to fix Natalie is like trying to part your hair without a mirror. It's impossible to know if you made a straighter part or a more crooked one.

I head back to my room and sift through the pile again. An old can of tooth powder, part of a shoelace, the back of a frame, and then my finger grazes something soft. A piece of her purple blanket!

I slip it in my pocket, a big grin on my face. I'll bring this to

Nat and miraculously she'll let go of the counting and rocking. She'll sleep easily each night. She'll make eye contact with everyone. And then I'll find out who or what started the fire, so that no one will suspect her again.

Sounds good, anyway. But dreams always do.

On the way out, I spot my blue homework notebook! The one with the essay in it. It's just sitting out here. That's strange. How could I have missed it before? I put the notebook under my arm and head back, an even bigger grin on my face. I won't have to do the paper again! Doing your homework twice is like puking, then having to eat your own vomit.

When I get home, I go straight to Nat's room to give her the piece of blanket, my chest puffed up with hope.

Nat takes the swatch of blanket and smells it. Then she hands it back to me.

"It doesn't smell right, does it . . . but Mom can wash it."

I close my hand over the little purple piece, then open it again, hoping she'll see it differently this time.

But of course that doesn't work.

I'm about to put the notebook with my stuff so I won't forget to take it to school, when I decide to flip through it to make sure it's all there. That's when I notice something strange.

On the top of the first page of my thesis about Roosevelt and his polio, it says *State problem* in handwriting that is hauntingly familiar.

Al Capone has sent me notes before. I know his handwriting really well.

But how did he get his hands on my homework? It must have been the cons who are working on our place. Somebody took my homework and gave it to him.

Except why'd he write that? *He* doesn't like my thesis? He's my English teacher now?

And then on the bottom of the last page he wrote:

Roosevelt is a good fella, but Capone is the guy you should be writing about. Okay, Roosevelt had that polio problem, but he was born rich. Capone started with nothing. He earned every penny himself.

Capone messed up my homework. How strange is that? A gangster did my homework. Not just any gangster, either—public enemy number one.

Luckily, he wrote in pencil.

14. Button It Up

Friday, January 24, 1936

On Friday morning when I'm getting ready for school, the phone rings at the Chudleys'. My mother and I stare at each other as if we are half expecting Mrs. Caconi to appear and answer it. Then Mom jumps up and rushes into the hallway to pick up the phone.

"Hello, this is Mrs. Helen Flanagan," she says awkwardly.

After a pause, her worry lines deepen. "Mr. Purdy, hello," she says. Mr. Purdy is the head of the Esther P. Marinoff School. Having the head of the school call you is never a good thing. But Natalie hasn't even been to school this week. How could she be in trouble?

My leg starts itching imagining the possibilities.

"Yes," my mother says.

"Well, now.

"But Mr.—

"Mr. Purdy, sir. You know that's not true.

"The board has no right to do that. Surely the insurance company won't suspend coverage based on an unfounded allegation."

I can only hear one side of the conversation, but one side is enough.

"That doesn't make sense." My mom is practically shouting into the phone.

"Temporarily meaning how long?

"The task force report. How do you know about that?

"Look, you can't make this decision without talking to us.

"Yes, but—

"Mr. Purdy—

"All right. Okay. I'll have my husband call you. But I know there's another way to handle this. It just isn't fair . . . she's been doing so well."

When my mother hangs up, she sits down on the crate we are using as a living room chair, her eyes on me. She lets her head fall into her hands.

"Mom," I say gently. "What did Mr. Purdy say?"

"The board is worried about the fire. They think Nat is a fire risk."

"That's ridiculous. They monitor her all the time there. Even if she were a fire risk, which she isn't, there's no way she could . . ."

"I know that, Moose." The vein in her forehead is pulsing. "But Mr. Purdy says we have to wait for the task force report. When they clear her, she can go back."

She shakes her head but doesn't lift it. "Do you know something about this, Moose?" she asks.

I'm surprised she asks this. How does she know? "Bea threatened to call the school."

My mother's jaw clenches. "I figured as much."

After a minute she stands up, takes a deep breath, and points to the phone. "This must work the same as the 64 building's, right?"

"I think so."

She nods. "I've got the number somewhere." She grabs her handbag and begins to dig through it.

"Who are you going to call?"

"Mrs. Kelly. She used to work at the Marinoff School. She knows Mr. Purdy. Maybe she can talk some sense into his head. She's due out here anyway. If I have to go one more night without sleep . . ." She sighs again. "I can't even think straight anymore."

That afternoon Mrs. Kelly is on the three o'clock boat.

"I'm sorry to hear about your apartment." She bustles into the Chudley kitchen. "And I did call Mr. Purdy and I let him know putting Natalie on probation, pending the task force report, is just plain ridiculous."

"Report should be out soon anyway," my father says. "Then we can put this all behind us."

Mrs. Kelly's lips pucker. In one sweep of her head, she takes in the dishes in the sink, the clothes on the chairs, the towels hung over the windows, and my parents' tired faces. She pulls up a crate and plunks herself on it. "What have you tried?"

My mother tells her about the warm milk before bed, the jumping rope, the hours of swinging Nat on the parade grounds, about sleeping in different beds, about the purple blanket swatch, and the new purple blanket that my father searched all of Union Square to find. And that's only what she can think of off the top of her head.

"Okay." Mrs. Kelly nods. "I get the picture. You guys going to stay here permanently?"

My father shakes his head. "Everybody liked our old place.

Should be able to move back in two weeks. Three at the most." My father looks around at the Chudleys', which appears to be occupied by messy campers. "Hauling all our stuff up here for two weeks didn't make sense."

"Two weeks is a long time to go without sleep," Mrs. Kelly says.

"I've got the crew working as fast as they can, but there was a lot of damage," my father tells her.

"Have you tried taking her button box?"

We all shake our heads. Nobody wants to take Nat's buttons away, mostly because more often than not, it actually makes matters worse.

"At least she's been quiet." My mother's voice is strained. "We're so close to the warden's house now. She pitches a fit and . . ."

"Ahhhck," Mrs. Kelly groans. She's heard enough. "Have you tried Moose's toothbrush?"

We nod.

"Let's rack our brains, people. I think the buttons are the answer. I'm just not sure how."

"I know." I raise one finger.

"Let's hear it," Mrs. Kelly commands, her palms up, her fingers wiggling like I should come out with it.

I look at my dad. "The button she gave you."

"What button . . . oh," Dad says. "My first day of work button."

"Do you have it?" my mom asks.

"Do you think I would lose ninety-seven? Whose father do you think I am, anyway?" He smiles as he reaches into his pocket for the simple, silver four-hole button.

"Let's get her in here. We'll make it a ceremony," Mrs. Kelly declares.

"What kind of a ceremony?"

"A button ceremony," she says.

Whatever that means. I can tell she's making this up as she goes along.

"What's the ceremony for?" I ask.

"What if she can't control whether she goes to sleep or not?" my mother squeaks.

"It will be like a talisman," Mrs. Kelly says. "Isn't that what it was for your dad? A good luck button?"

We nod.

"Then this use will be consistent with the button's previous symbolism."

She can't be serious. If I wasn't so desperate, I'd laugh.

"Let's tell her you're going to give her the button at night, and in the morning you'll take it back. She's not to have it during the day for any reason.

"Moose, you'll get down on your knees. And hand her the button like it's a diamond ring," Mrs. Kelly says.

"She's my sister. I'm not proposing to her."

"I'll do it," my dad jumps in. My mom hands him a folded towel and he puts the button on top and we all trudge into Nat's Chudley room.

"Okay, sweet pea," he says. "I didn't want to have to do this. But I don't see any other way. I'm going to have to give you your button back."

This gets Nat's attention. Her eyes rove across my father. "I like having it in my pocket," he continues, "but you need it so you can sleep at night."

"Sleep at night," Nat says.

"That's right," my father says. "Where do you want me to put it?"

"In my room," she says loudly and clearly.

"Okey dokey then," he says, placing the button on the milk carton table by her bed.

"No, *my* room. Number 2E." Nat cries, "My room, 2E!"

"Natalie's Chudley room," Mrs. Kelly says.

"Number 2E, 2E," Nat belts out.

"We'll be back to number 2E soon, but Nat, they have to get it fixed up. They can't work on it with us underfoot." My father is still on his hands and knees. He looks like he's pleading with her now.

"No wait, Dad. Nat's right. We should listen to her. We could do this, you know. We could take our blankets and pillows down to 2E."

"Number 2E," Nat says. "Buttons in 2E. Sleep in 2E."

"We could live up here and when it's time to go to bed, head down to 64," I say.

"Bea Trixle will have a conniption," my mother says.

"She's going to have a conniption when we move back anyway. May as well get it over with," I say.

"Who would you rather have pitch a fit, Helen . . . this Trixle woman or Natalie?" Mrs. Kelly asks.

"Bea Trixle," I say.

My mother sits transfixed for a moment. But then she nods her head. "Moose is right. When you pitch a fit, it puts you one down, no matter who you are. Better Bea Trixle than Natalie."

"I like the way you're thinking, Moose," Mrs. Kelly tells me.

"And by the way, how's the work on your sister's eye contact coming along?"

Mrs. Kelly just never lets up, does she? We haven't even solved this crisis and she's already on to the next.

"Working on it," I mumble.

That night when it's bedtime, we all gather our blankets and traipse down to 64 building. Nat puts Dad's good luck button and the swatch of blanket in her button box. She also has my baseball glove. I don't know how she got that again, but I'm not going to cross her right now.

We watch as she climbs in her bed. There are no sheets, no pillow. She can't wait for any of that. Within minutes she's snoring.

"We should have listened to Natalie," I whisper. "That's what she was saying all along."

My father shakes his head. "Don't I know it," he says, reaching for Mom's hand.

15. The Chinless Man

Saturday, January 25, 1936

The next day I peek in at the cockroaches in their cardboard home on top of the bookshelf in Jimmy and Theresa's room. I can't believe I'm relying on ten greasy bugs.

"Don't do anything without me," Theresa warns Jimmy, Annie, and me as we hover around the cockroaches.

Jimmy squints at Theresa. "Where are you going?"

"I got to work for Piper this morning," Theresa reports.

"We're doing this now," Jimmy informs her. "You want to be a part, you have to stay."

Theresa crosses her arms and stamps her foot, her bottom lip puckered out. "Nuts," she says.

"Why isn't Piper coming down, anyway?" Jimmy asks. "Doesn't she know we're running the cockroaches today?"

"She said to let her know if it got interesting," Annie says.

"Not everyone thinks cockroaches are as much fun as you do," I tell Jimmy.

"Their loss," Jimmy tells me as a cockroach crawls up his arm.

"What's the plan, anyway?" I ask.

"We got to watch the dock guards, first thing. We can't do this when they're paying attention," Jimmy says, moving the cockroach from his armpit back down to his wrist again.

"Or we'll get in trouble," Annie says.

"Right." Jimmy nods.

"Is Trixle on duty?" I ask.

"Yeah. My dad is too, for part of the time," Annie says. I give Annie a second look. It's hard to get used to tall and thin Annie when she's always been squat and sturdy Annie.

"What are we watching for?" I ask Jimmy.

"We got to see when the guards turn their backs," he says, taking a second cockroach out of the box and letting it scamper up his other arm.

"I don't know, you guys. Maybe we shouldn't . . ." Annie says.

"What's the harm?" Jimmy asks. "We aren't getting near the cons, the cockroaches are."

Annie crosses her arms in front of her chest and raises her blond eyebrows. "It's not your dad working today."

"What's that got to do with anything?" Jimmy asks.

Annie frowns. Her eyes focus on the bottle cap curtain, which separates Theresa's side of the room from Jimmy's.

"Annie," I say, "if you don't want to do this, you don't have to."

Jimmy and I exchange a look. Annie doesn't like to do things that might possibly be against a rule the adults haven't thought to make yet. We wait for her to say something else, but she doesn't.

"So where should we go?" I ask.

"Best view is from the balcony," Jimmy says, capturing both cockroaches and putting them back in the box.

"And remind me why exactly we're doing this?" Annie asks.

"We're hoping the cons won't be able to resist the opportunity to brag," I say.

"But we can't just stand on the balcony gawking at the cons," Annie says.

Jimmy takes the cockroach box under his arm. "Don't worry, I've got it all figured out," he says as we head through the Mattaman living room to the front balcony.

Annie stands watching us, her mouth open, ready to object. I think she's not going to come, but when I look back, there she is.

Jimmy heads for the balcony right outside his apartment. We sit cross-legged in a semicircle by the railing. Jimmy takes out a piece of paper and folds it up into a triangle and we play a lame game of flick the paper football. "We have to pretend to be busy," he whispers.

It doesn't take long before Indiana, the guy with no eyebrows, notices us.

"Morrrrrrrning Annie, Jimmy, Mooooooose," he calls out, waving with both hands, like he's washing windows with two hands at once.

We don't answer.

"Who wants to say good morning to someone that creepy?" Annie whispers.

"It's his eyebrows," I say. "He must shave them off."

"I wonder what he does with the eyebrow hairs?" Jimmy asks.

"Seems like you need a special place for eyebrow hairs," I say.

"An eyebrow hair receptacle," Jimmy adds.

"Exactly," I laugh.

"You know, this really isn't something I want to think about," Annie says.

"The problem is his chin, anyway," Jimmy says.

"He has no chin," I say.

"That's the problem," Jimmy agrees.

"Never trust a man with no chin." Me again.

"Even if he had eyebrows and a chin, he'd still be creepy," Annie decides.

There's no way the cons can hear us, but something about how they're watching is disturbing, like they're better at this than we are. "C'mon you guys, we have to move. We're too visible," Annie mutters.

"Let's try the corner by the stairwell," I say.

"Too far away. We won't be able to see the cockroach from there," Annie says.

"Let's just stay here. They'll forget about us," Jimmy says.

Jimmy's right, they get bored of us and go back to work. Which is the good news and the bad news, because now watching them is as exciting as observing the currents in the bay. Who cares?

But then slowly I begin to notice little things. Lizard, Indiana, and Count Lustig are friends and they're always nodding to each other, sweeping next to one another, and saving each other a place in line. When Indiana is in the back of the pickup, Lizard is the one tossing laundry bags to him. When the Count is planting flowers by the switchback, Lizard is carrying the potting soil.

Indiana is the weirdest of the three, but Lizard is a close second with his big fleshy face and skinny legs. The Count looks perfectly normal. Normal height. Normal posture. Normal brown hair. He blends in. You would never pick him out of a crowd.

When the count bell rings, the cons line up. Then Trixle

comes by and counts them himself or sometimes he has them count off. This is to make sure no prisoner has escaped. He reports the count to the dock officer, the dock officer writes it on a slip of paper, then he attaches the paper to a guy-wire at the bottom of the dock tower. The tower officer operates the pulley, and the message zips up the fifty feet to the tower. Then the tower officer calls in the count to the control room in the cell house.

The whole transaction takes five minutes, sometimes longer—depending on who is on dock duty. If it's someone Trixle likes, he takes a cigarette break and they discuss the Seals game or some boxer guy like Baby Arizmendi.

"Jimmy, let's send our bug man out," I whisper as the balcony shakes with the clickety-clackety of high heels.

"Mr. Mattaman," Bea Trixle shouts down.

Jimmy's head pops up. "Yes, ma'am." He swivels toward the sound of Bea's voice.

Clickety-clackety. Bea appears. She's breathing hard, teetering on her high heels, which, so far as I know, she never takes off. Even her slippers have high heels on them. She shakes her finger at Jimmy. "How dare you?"

"How dare I what?" Jimmy asks.

"Did you think I wouldn't notice?"

"Wouldn't notice what, ma'am?" he asks politely.

"Fifty dollars has up and gone. *Fifty* dollars!"

"I don't know what you're talking about, ma'am," Jimmy says.

"Don't lie to me, Jimmy. The money is gone and you're the only one who could have touched it."

"That's nuts," Jimmy says, looking her straight in the eye.

"I've never stolen one penny in my whole life. Not from you. Not from anyone."

Her face softens with doubt, but then she revs up for a second round. "I took you into my store because your folks needed money. I gave you a job and this is what you do to me?"

Jimmy stands firm. "I'm not a thief."

"Moose here probably put you up to it. I'm going to tell the warden and call the police. Let them sort it out. You watch me!"

"Mrs. Trixle, ma'am, I didn't take your money." His voice doesn't waver.

"And I didn't put him up to it," I say.

"The least you can do is be a man and fess up." Her eyes are trained on Jimmy.

"Nothing to confess. I—didn't—take—your—money," Jimmy repeats slowly, as if she doesn't speak English.

"I will expect you to pay it back, do you hear me? But not from working at my store. No sirree, buster. *You* are fired."

"That's crazy talk, ma'am. You can't accuse me like this." Jimmy looks at her, his face full of defiance.

"Oh yeah? You watch me." She turns on her heels and clickety-clacks back across the balcony.

My mouth hangs open. Annie's eyes pop out of her head. "What was that all about?" she asks.

Jimmy flaps his hand like it isn't a big deal.

"Are you kidding me? She accused you of being a thief," I say.

He shrugs. "She does it all the time. She makes mistakes with her bookkeeping, then she claims I'm stealing from her."

"But fifty dollars . . ."

"It's never been that much before," he agrees. "Once it was

two dollars. Once eleven fifty. Another time twenty. She's a barrel of laughs to work for, I'm telling you," he says, though his voice has a catch in it—like what just happened is starting to sink in.

"You lost your job," I say.

He shrugs. "She always hires me back. She can't run the place without me."

"Does she ever apologize?" Annie asks.

"She brings me up a piece of pie, then mumbles about there being a mistake in the books. Never that she makes the mistake. The books were mistaken." He smiles. "Then she says: 'See you tomorrow?'"

"And you say yes?"

"You see a lot of jobs on this island for kids? I earn half my mom's grocery money," Jimmy says as Mrs. Caconi wheezes past us on the balcony. The smell of baking powder and sweat fills the air.

I shake my head. "Still," I whisper, "you'd better go talk to your mom. Bea said she was calling the police."

He sighs. "She'll never do it. It will make her look like a fool when they discover it's a bookkeeping error. I'll tell my mom as soon as we're done. Let's get our cockroach out there."

"Jimmy," I whisper, "you don't think the missing money could be related to the fire in some way?"

Jimmy jumps up. "She probably added wrong. That's what she always does. C'mon, if we're going to do this, we better get on it before they go to lunch."

"So what are we going to ask them? The cons, I mean," Annie asks.

"What they know about the fire," Jimmy explains. "My dad says they know everything that happens on this island."

"People always say that, but I wonder if it's true," Annie says.

"You have another idea?" Jimmy asks.

Annie shakes her head.

"Let's just ask flat out," I say.

What do you know about the fire? Annie writes because she has the best handwriting.

I roll the note into a tight cylinder. Jimmy takes thread and ties the roll, like a diploma, then secures it to the cockroach's back. It's amazing how good he is at this, like he's been tying messages to cockroaches his whole life. "We need to target one of the convicts. Which one do you think?"

"The Count," Annie says.

"He's the most normal," I say, rearranging my legs, which are cramped from sitting for so long.

"Okay, Count Lustig, then," Jimmy says. "When Trixle finishes with the convict count, I'll give the sign and we'll go."

I keep one eye on Trixle moving through the men and one eye on Jimmy. When Jimmy nods, I spring into action, fast-walking across the balcony and down the stairs. On the dock level, I toss a chunk of cookie. It lands near Count Lustig. He glances at the cookie, but doesn't reach for it. He goes about his business scrubbing the deck.

I run across, sticking close to the front of 64, then toss another cookie chunk between Jimmy and the Count. Jimmy releases the cockroach. The cockroach stands still.

We hold our breath, looking from the cockroach to Trixle and back again. Then our cockroach scuttles forward.

Lizard has the soapy water bucket against his big chest. The Count motions toward the bug. The cockroach zigs and zags toward the Count.

Darby pats his pocket for his cigarettes, then digs his fingers inside. He takes the cigarette out and strikes the match, inhaling deeply.

The cockroach darts out to the first cookie crumb.

Most of the cons are watching the cockroach. Do they see the tiny scroll on its back?

The cockroach seems content with one cookie crumb. It scoots toward the shade of 64 building.

I run back up to Annie. Jimmy is already there. His lip is twisted, his face full of disappointment. This isn't going to work and he knows it.

Trixle and Annie's dad reach a lag in their discussion. Trixle turns to check on the cons. "Get to work," he barks, then he's back talking to Bomini again.

Lizard dunks his scrub brush in his bucket, then crawls on his hands and knees toward the cockroach.

Annie darts a hopeful look at me.

Lizard is rapidly overtaking the cockroach. His hand hovers and then shoots out, snatching the brown bug.

"Yes!" I whisper as Lizard dangles the cockroach in front of his face, then pops it in his mouth, note and all, his Adam's apple slipping up and down his throat.

"Oh my God! He ate the cockroach," Annie says.

Lizard smiles up at us, then he rubs his belly as if he's just eaten a satisfying meal.

Indiana's laugh cuts through the air.

Trixle whips around, dropping his cigarette before he's half done and grinding it out with his shoe. "What's your problem, 141?" he asks.

The entire work crew is looking at us.

"All right . . ." Darby barks. "What's going on here, folks?"

Nobody answers.

"Moose." He motions me to come down.

Why is it always me? I glance back at Jimmy and Annie as I trudge down to Darby.

"What have you guys been doing up there for so long?" Darby demands.

"Catching cockroaches, sir," I tell him when I'm down on the dock, careful to stay on my side of the white line.

"Catching cockroaches, my foot." Darby has his bullhorn now, his voice amplified. "You kids are up to no good. You think the rules don't apply to you, well, I got news for you."

Seems to me the opposite is true. The rules apply even more to me. He's singled me out *because* my dad is the associate warden, but I manage to keep this to myself.

"You can't encourage these jokers." Trixle nods toward the cons. "You gotta let them know who's boss. Don't suppose you've learned *that* from your daddy. They eat you alive if you're too nice, but no. Cam Flanagan gets promoted. Warden Williams ought to have his head examined."

"Don't talk about my dad or the warden that way." My voice vibrates like an eggbeater. I should not be talking back to an adult and I know it.

"That's right, your daddy is the boss now, isn't he? Shall I march you up to the warden's place so you can explain why you're hanging around down here, sticking your nose where it don't belong?" Trixle's eyes drill into me.

"No, sir."

"All righty then. I'd keep my mouth shut if I were you. Far as you know, I'm respectful of your father and the warden . . . you hear?"

"Yes, sir," I say.

"Glad we understand each other . . . Now get outta here. I don't want to see your face up on the balcony, the stairwell, nowhere around here, unless you are on your way somewhere else, understood?"

I glance at the cons. They're all standing in line now, waiting to go back up the switchback. Darby didn't tell them to do this, they just did.

Darby's bullhorn is at the ready two inches from his lips, but there's nothing he can say to chew them out. He moves from one foot to the other like he's got blisters on his toes.

The cons got the best of him, just as they got the best of Jimmy and Annie and me.

They're obedient and defiant. How can that be?

16. One Thing You Shouldn't Do

Wednesday, January 29, 1936

So much for the cockroach plan. I wonder if it's dead yet or if it's crawling around inside Lizard. Can a cockroach survive the digestive process?

Everybody's been so busy this week; it's now Wednesday and still we haven't made our next move. I'm starting to get antsy. Jimmy and Annie had to go into the city with their moms this afternoon. I have to watch Natalie so my mother can teach a piano lesson to one of the little boys who lives on the island.

"Bye, Mom," I tell her as she sails out the door to the Officers' Club, her music bag biting into her shoulder. Nat is busy manning the light switch, on-off, on-off.

With my mom gone, I can't help thinking of Mrs. Kelly and how I told her I was working on the eye contact problem.

I take a page and write *47 times 234* on it and tape it to my forehead.

"How much is it?" I ask.

Nat's eyes brush past my face. "Ten thousand, nine hundred and ninety-eight," she says. She somehow has managed to take in the numbers that quick.

I tape a new page up to my forehead. "Look in my eyes," I tell her.

Again, the numbers seem to enter her brain without her ever looking at them. I try a harder equation to slow her down: *56,478 x 43 = ?*

"Hey Nat, what's this?"

"Two million, four hundred and twenty-eight thousand, five hundred and fifty-four," she answers. I don't need to check if she's right. She's always right.

Nat is headed for the closet now. She finds her shoes and puts her toes in them, but not her heels.

"We aren't going out, Nat," I say.

"I—am—going—outside," she says, each word pronounced more carefully than the last.

I jump in front of her, blocking the door. "Look here." I point to my forehead, where I am holding a new equation—it's faster than taping it.

"Five million, three hundred and twenty-one thousand, seven," she says. "Moose stay. I go."

"No, you can't go by yourself."

"I go," she repeats.

"You can't, Natalie."

She shakes her head hard.

"I go," she repeats.

"I'm babysitting. You can't go."

"I'm older," she blurts out.

"Yeah, I know, but . . ."

"I am older!" she shouts.

"Okay, all right, you're older." I stuff my feet into my shoes, wiggle them on without undoing the laces. "Where are we going?" I ask.

"The birds," Nat says. "Moose get the bread."

Nat loves to feed the birds. My dad likes to take her down to the dock with a few crusts of bread.

There isn't any stale bread, so I bring three fresh slices and some crackers. Nat waits patiently for me, but when I open the door, she pushes in front. I hurry to pass her. She stops in her tracks.

"I am older," she insists. Natalie always wins.

I feel like a chump following her, but there's nothing left to do. I can't have her pitching a fit.

When we get down to the dock, the birds all seem to know Natalie. They're like noisy kids waiting for her. Their squawking rises to a fevered pitch, then dies down in a rolling rhythm like the surf.

Nat takes the bread and begins her ritual. Each slice must be broken into a certain number of pieces and then the pieces thrown so that they get divided evenly among the birds.

Natalie is in charge. She doesn't need me. I watch for a while, but I get tired of how relentlessly methodical Natalie is and I begin pacing, drifting farther and farther away, until I'm outside the Caconis' apartment on the ground floor of 64. The Caconis' apartment is dark and quiet. The only sign of life is the laundry bag sitting on the doormat. That's when I start thinking about what happened with Donny Caconi and the bottle cap and how Jimmy didn't believe Donny could throw better than I could and he wasn't even there. How did he win?

Maybe I'm just a sore loser, but I can't help wondering if you could doctor bottle caps so that one flew better than the other. Would Donny's pockets have a clue?

I look out at Nat. The birds are winding down. They know

when she's run out of bread. I wave to Nat to come back. It doesn't look like she sees me, but she must, because she starts walking my way.

I pick up the laundry bag. "Let's go," I say.

"No Moose. Caconi. Not Flanagan," she murmurs like she thinks I'm playing the Stupid Moose game.

"Yeah I know, Nat. I'm just checking something."

"Caconi. Not Flanagan," Nat says louder this time.

"I'll bring it right back," I assure her.

My father once told me there are lots of things to keep private, but if you're doing something in secret ask yourself why.

His voice keeps rattling around in my head, but my hands still have the Caconi laundry bag and my legs are following Nat up the stairs. Inside #2E, I head straight for my room. On the way, I flick the hall light switch a few times. It doesn't even work right now, but Nat's happy turning it on and off anyway. I slip in my room and close the door.

My pulse beats in my head like the tommy guns on the officers' firing range. I reach in the bag and pull out one of Mrs. Caconi's aprons.

That's strange. She doesn't send her laundry through. She doesn't like having the convicts touch her clothes.

I rifle through Donny's pants, his shirts, his socks. I wiggle my hand inside each pocket. Empty. Empty. Empty. Every pocket is empty.

Did I really think Donny Caconi was a cheat? Now I'm ashamed of myself.

I'm just putting Mrs. Caconi's gigantic apron back in the bag when I feel something hard graze my hand.

Inside her apron pocket is a handkerchief with something inside.

A round roll of money. Five-dollar bills. Eight of them. Forty dollars!

Mrs. Caconi is not rich. Why would she leave forty dollars in her pocket?

17. Fingering Suckers

Wednesday, January 29, 1936

I can't do anything about the money. I mean really, what am I going to do? I'd have to tell my dad I was rifling through Donny's pockets because I didn't believe he could outthrow me.

What does that make me look like?

A chump.

I think about telling Jimmy. But I can't do that, either. I mean, I didn't even find anything, except money. It isn't a crime to leave money in your pocket—even if it is a lot of money. But if the laundry cons find it, she'll lose it for sure. How do I explain to Mrs. Caconi how I happened to be digging through her pocket?

It seems like the best thing to do is leave well enough alone. I put the money back where I found it and shove the Caconis' laundry bag inside ours.

"C'mon, Nat," I say.

"Where c'mon?" she asks.

"You were right. Caconi, not Flanagan. This isn't our laundry bag. We're going to return it."

"Just checking something," she mumbles.

"Yeah, I know. I checked and now it's time to put it back."

Natalie nods and follows along behind me without any

argument. She likes putting things back where they belong.

To my surprise, the dock cons are out. They usually don't come down in the afternoon, but I guess the ferry dropped off a lot of building supplies for #2E. Darby must have decided it was easier to bring the cons down than have the officers move all that lumber up two flights of stairs.

I dig the Caconis' laundry bag out of ours, and drop it where I found it. As soon as I've let it go, I begin to breathe more normally again.

Nat and I stand behind the white line watching the cons. Lizard can't seem to do anything without talking to Indiana about it. The Count takes orders from Indiana too, but he clearly doesn't like this. The way he clears his throat and purses his lips makes me wonder if Indiana gets on his nerves.

The cons are in a line formation, carrying lumber off the ferry, when I see Indiana flick his head like he wants something. Lizard moves forward to talk to Darby, while the Count slips to the rain gutter, kneels down, takes off his shoe, and shakes it as if he's got a pebble inside.

This would look perfectly normal if I hadn't seen that nod between Indiana and Count Lustig. It reminds me of the code between the catcher and the pitcher about what kind of pitch to throw. Plus it seems like Lizard's trying to distract Darby.

Now the Count's got his hand in the downspout. Did he put something in? Or take something out?

The whole thing takes maybe thirty seconds and then the Count slides back in line and Lizard finishes talking to Darby. Now Lizard and the Count are carrying the two-by-fours up the stairwell, as if nothing happened.

What the heck was that about?

I could just walk right over there and find out.

"Wait here a second," I tell Natalie as I walk by the downspout and kneel down. I'm pretending to retie my shoe—with one hand, while the other reaches inside the rain gutter. I pull out a leaf and a small piece of paper folded up tight like a football. I slip the paper in my pocket and tie my shoe just as I hear the cons coming down the stairwell again

"C'mon, Nat," I say. We take the other stairwell up and across to the back of 64. My hand shakes as I unfold the paper. It has numbers on it.

(213) 35-2-75

A code? An address? Part of a phone number? Alcatraz convict numbers?

Nat is walking on toward the swings. I run to catch up with her, then show her the slip of paper. "What do you make of this?"

She drags her toe against the ground, her complete attention on that foot.

"You don't know?" I ask.

"Don't know," she mutters.

"Yeah, me neither," I tell her.

I try to think this through. If the Count put this information in the rain gutter, he's trying to communicate these numbers—whatever they are—to someone.

But isn't this a bad spot to put a message for another prisoner? Wouldn't it be easier to send messages in the cell house?

What if this isn't a message for another convict.

What if it's a message for one of us.

That's when I begin to itch all over.

Now I know I need to talk to Annie and Jimmy. I tell Natalie she'll get extra swing time after we talk to Annie, and to my surprise, Natalie follows along without any objection.

When Annie opens the door, she blushes so deeply, it looks like she's rolled her cheeks in pomegranate juice.

Her hair is wet and she has her bathrobe on.

I'm so keyed up, I can hardly get the story out.

"Show me," Annie says when I'm done, and I dig the note out of my pocket.

"Chapters or page numbers? Geometry? Coordinates? Longitude and latitude? It could be anything," she says.

"Only one way to find out."

"Which is?" Annie asks.

"Put it back and see who picks it up."

"Watch the downspout all the time? How are we going to do that? And besides, won't that be dangerous?"

"Not if they don't see us. Listen Annie, what do you know about the Count?"

"You heard about his Eiffel Tower con, right?"

"The one where he sold it?"

"Uh-huh, as scrap metal to a scrap metal company. Played that scam twice. He likes to forge things too. Hey wait a minute. Theresa and I made a convict card for him. I'll go get it."

She and Theresa make these convict cards for the best-known cons. Annie does the research and Theresa helps her write up the cards. They're recipe cards folded in quarters.

Count Lustig, AKA: Victor Lustig, Robert V. Miller, Victor Gross, Albert Phillips, Charles Gruber, George Shobo, Robert Lamar, JR Richards,

Victor Shaffer, Frank Hessler, Frank Kessler

Born in: Bohemia

Family: Wife and daughter

Business: Con artist

Favorite pastime: Reading.

"Reading? That's his hobby?"
Annie shrugs.

Favorite crime: The Count stole $22,000 from a group of bankers. When they caught up with him, he convinced them if they pressed charges, their bank would go belly up. The bankers let him go free and paid him $1,000 for the inconvenience they caused.

"So wait . . . he blackmailed them about his own crime?"
"Yep."
"That's one for the record books."

Favorite description of crimes: "Fingering suckers"

Most famous escape attempt: The Count escaped from prison in New York City by weaving bed linens into a rope. He cut the wire screen in the bathroom with stolen wire cutters and lowered himself down three stories on the woven bedsheet rope.

Sent to jail for: Running a confidence or "Bunco" game

Current home: Alcatraz Island

"I know, I'm gonna get my baseball gear. I left it at the Mattamans'. We'll play catch at the dock and just happen to drop the ball around the gutter. And then I'll put the note back."

Annie gives me a funny look. "Moose?"

"What?" I ask, my hand on the door.

"I'm in my bathrobe."

My ears heat up.

Natalie laughs. I turn and watch her. She actually got the humor.

"She likes to make fun of you, Moose, that's for sure. Look, I have to get ready. We'll put it back tomorrow, okay?" Annie smiles.

It takes me by surprise that smile . . . how beautiful it is.

On my way across the balcony, I do some thinking. What if whoever is expecting to find the note looks for it and it isn't there? Will he get suspicious and change the drop location? That would be bad for us because we wouldn't know the new location.

I should put the note back now, but I doubt I'll be able to get Natalie to go down there again. I can only put off her swing time for so long.

"Nat," I say when we get to the stairwell. "Let's go the long way to the parade grounds."

"Short way," Nat says.

"If we go the long way, we can check on your birds," I say.

"No bread," Nat says.

"I know, but still. The long way. Just this once?"

"Two hours," she says.

"It doesn't take two hours. It's an extra five minutes, that's all."

"Two hours at the swings," she says.

"Two hours!" I laugh. She's got me over a barrel and she knows it.

"Okay." I put my hands up. "Two hours."

I have to put the note back, but the cons are still in #2E. I stall until I see Darby march them back up the hill to the cell house. Then we bypass the second floor and go directly to the dock again, where I follow the same trick tying my shoe by the downspout. Only this time I return the folded note to its original hiding place.

Now all I have to do is watch.

Except first I have to give Natalie her swing time at the parade grounds or there's going to be big trouble.

Natalie walks faster and faster the closer we get. But when we come around the bend and have a clear view of the swings, we see Nat's favorite swing is occupied by Janet Trixle.

"Nat, take the other swing. It's much better. I've tried it," I say, though even as the words come out of my mouth, I know this is futile. Natalie only likes the one swing. She'll wait hours for it to be free.

Sure enough, when we get there, Nat lines up behind Janet waiting for her turn.

"Nat." I jiggle the chains on the open swing. "You can swing here until your swing is available."

But Nat won't fall for this. I've tried it before.

"Janet," I say. "Would you mind switching? Natalie really likes the swing you're on."

Janet digs her toe in the sand to stop herself. She stands up holding tight to the swing chains. "I can't," she says.

"Why not?" I ask.

"My mom." She frowns, nodding in the direction of Bea Trixle, who is headed our way.

Oh, great . . . now I want to get out of here, but there's no way to persuade Natalie. I promised her two hours. It's amazing she let me put her off as much as I have already. Nat rocks, hovering behind Janet's swing. She waits to pounce the second Janet lets it go.

Blickety-blackety. Bea's high heels make a dull sound on the cement. "What did Daddy tell you about standing your ground, Janet," Bea Trixle asks, clutching her fur-trimmed sweater. "You can't let big kids push you around."

Janet scoots back on her swing. "Sorry," she tells me.

"Janet Lily Trixle." Bea scowls. "Why are *you* apologizing? The Flanagan girl has no business here. We should post a sign. These swings are meant for children ten and under."

"No business here." Natalie wedges the sand between her feet.

"You have to be tough in this world, Janet, or people will take advantage of you," Bea rattles on.

Janet inspects her feet. "The pixies find things in the sand. Valuable things like jewels," she whispers.

"Not the pixies again," Bea snaps.

"I mean me. I find things in the sand," Janet corrects herself.

"Janet Trixle," Darby's bullhorn booms across the parade grounds. "Attention!"

Janet jumps out of her swing, then stands up straight as a ship's mast.

"Do you have your bullhorn, Lieutenant?" Darby asks.

"Yes, sir," Janet says, pulling a Janet-size bullhorn out of her pixie bag. She holds it in her right hand, like Darby does, and follows in lockstep behind him. Bea glares at me, dumps the sand from her high heels, and blickety-blacks after them.

With Janet gone, Nat slides into her favorite swing. It's started to drizzle now. In a few minutes, it's really raining, but even if it starts to pour, I have to let Nat swing the full two hours. A promise is a promise.

The rain gains force, pelting our heads. The wind stings our faces, but Nat continues swinging happily. She doesn't care that she's soaking wet.

The water has begun to drip off my nose by the time it occurs to me that a paper note in the downspout won't last long in rain like this.

18. Flickering Lights

Thursday, January 30, 1936

The next day I'm on the late ferry after my baseball game when I see Mr. Mattaman and Mr. Bomini come up the gangway. Normally I wouldn't eavesdrop, but I don't have any leads on the fire, and even if the note was somehow involved, it's washed away now. I walk all the way around the ferry to the other side, where I can hear their conversation without them knowing I'm there. It will probably be nothing, but you never can tell.

I hold on to the railings as the boat picks up speed. I'm only half paying attention when Mr. Mattaman says:

"How's that hand healing anyway?"

"Doin' fine. Probably have some scarring, but it's not like I'm all that pretty anyway." Bomini laughs.

"Task force sure is taking their sweet time," Mattaman says.

"Bureaucracy in action."

"Been nearly two weeks, hasn't it? When's it supposed to come out?"

"I have no idea," Mr. Bomini says.

"Having it up in the air like this isn't helping matters."

"Tell me about it."

"Trixle's dead sure it was Natalie and he's got a lot of folks nodding their heads right alongside him. Bit of a witch hunt, it seems to me," Mattaman says.

"I know it's possible, but I sure hope it isn't true."

"Sure puts Cam in a bad spot. And Trixle is milking that for all it's worth."

"People pointing fingers . . . it's bound to get ugly," Mr. Mattaman says.

"I heard they're going to haul Capone in there. Give him the third degree."

"They give him too much credit. He thinks he knows everything as it is."

"It does make them seem desperate," Bomini says.

"Reports for the bureau always got to have all the *i*'s dotted and the *t*'s crossed."

"Better safe than sorry," Mr. Bomini says as the ferry pitches in the wake of a steamer ship.

"Had an incident in the laundry yesterday that was mighty curious. I caught the Count giving Lizard five bucks."

"Five bucks. How'd he get that?"

"Beats me. But when I called him on it—"

"Don't tell me . . . he swallowed it."

"How'd you know?"

"That guy will eat anything. I've seen him eat a book. Cover and all."

"You don't think he's going to be watching for the fiver out the other end . . . do you?"

"Not much else to do in those cells." Bo Bomini laughs as the *Coxe* approaches the dock, cutting across the white foam, which looks like a giant glob of spit on the water.

"Probably something simple started that fire. A busted

circuit maybe. We get the task force report, everything will settle down."

"I dunno," Mattaman says as the bosun wraps the line around the cleat. "Something doesn't smell right and it's not only this fire business."

My shoulders hunch forward, the good mood drained right out of me. I keep trying to push the idea that Nat could have started the fire out of my mind and it keeps coming back again.

I wait until Bomini and Mattaman are off the boat before I cross the swaying gangplank. Annie is waiting on the other side. She takes one look at me and knows something's wrong. "What's up?" she asks.

"People still think it was Natalie that started the fire."

She waggles her head around in a way that says *Well yeah, of course*. "But Moose, I've been thinking a lot about this. C'mon, let's go somewhere we can talk."

"Up by the eucalyptus trees?"

Annie nods and we hike around the south end of the island and then up the hill to the small grove of eucalyptus trees.

We sit down on the side of the hill, which looks across to Treasure Island and the city. "Tell me again what happened that night," Annie says.

"Do I have to?"

She nods.

"Natalie was in my room. I made a bed for her on the floor, like I always do when I babysit."

"When you woke up, was she asleep?"

I dig a rock out of the hillside and toss it in the water. "I don't know."

Annie nods. "Was the light on?" she asks.

"In my room?"

"Or anywhere else?"

"The light was on in my room because I didn't mean to fall asleep. But everywhere else the lights were off. My dad is a stickler about that. He can't stand when we waste electricity."

"So the light in the kitchen wasn't on? You're sure?" Annie asks.

"I'm the son of an electrician. I don't leave the lights on."

"Wouldn't Natalie have to turn the light on to see the stove?" Annie persists.

"I guess so . . . Oh my God. Annie!" I jump up, sending a landslide of dirt down the hill.

She nods, a smile spreading across her face.

"Once Nat starts with the lights, she doesn't stop. She'd stand there all night flicking them off and on. Off and on. She wouldn't have gone to the stove. She'd never have made it there." Relief shoots through me like I've been holding my breath for weeks.

"It wasn't Natalie," I say. I almost hug Annie then. I can't believe she thought of this.

"Now we know for sure," Annie says. She stands up and brushes her skirt off.

"Let's go find Jimmy. We got to tell him about this.

"Annie?" I say as we tromp back down the path and around to 64 again.

"Yes?" She glances back at me.

"Thank you."

"Sure," she mumbles, crossing her arms in front of her chest and holding them tight.

• • •

At the Mattamans', Jimmy is in his room. We knock and he comes out, closing the door behind him as if whatever he's working on in there, he doesn't want us to see.

He looks from me to Annie and back again. "You know something," he guesses.

"Yeah." I smile big as the Golden Gate.

Annie fills him in on the details.

"No kidding," he says. "That's great news."

Then I let them know what I heard their dads talking about on the boat.

"I wish we could know what's on the task force report before the results are announced," Jimmy says.

"They're going to question Capone. Maybe we can hear what he says," I suggest.

"If it's in the cell house, we wouldn't stand a chance of getting in," Jimmy says.

"It's not going to be the cell house," I say.

"Why not?" Annie asks.

"It would make him a target. If the other cons know he's being questioned, then somebody gets accused, they'll think he's a snitch and beat the crap out of him," I say.

"Nobody's going to think Al Capone is a snitch," Annie says.

"Why not?" I ask.

"Because he's Al Capone," Annie says.

"I'm not sure they care," I say. "In fact, it might make him a bigger target."

"No matter what, Piper's the person to talk to. She'll know what the plan is," Jimmy says.

"When you talk to her, will you find out what's up? She's been acting strange," Annie says.

"When *I* talk to her?" I say.

Jimmy and Annie are both nodding now. "You know she likes you best. Although she did buy Annie a brand-new baseball. I saw her leave a gift for Donny, too."

"What's with all the gifts?"

"I dunno. She told me I was a good friend and she wanted me to know it," Annie chimes in. "She's never said I was a good friend before. She's never said I was a friend at all. And then she got choked up."

"She was faking," I say.

"Seemed real to me," Annie says.

"Plus Theresa made three dollars last week!" Jimmy says. "It takes me a month to earn three bucks worth of grocery credit. And that's a real job."

"Piper's grandma," I say. "She has money."

"But she's never had money like this before," Annie says.

I look at Annie. "See, you have information I don't. You should come with me."

Annie shakes her head.

"C'mon. She didn't give *me* a baseball."

"I already tried talking to her, but I didn't get anywhere," Annie says.

"Okay, okay, but then you guys are in charge of the downspout. We have to find out who is using that as a drop."

"Don't worry Moose, we've been watching," Jimmy says.

When I get to the warden's house and ring the bell, he answers the door himself.

"Good afternoon, sir," I say.

"Young Mr. Flanagan . . . to what do we owe the pleasure of your company?"

See, this is the problem with the warden right here. Is this sarcasm or not?

"I wanted to say hello to Piper," I say.

"You do, do you?"

"Yes, sir," I say.

"Well, go on up, then," he tells me, and I make a beeline for Piper's room.

"Yeah. Come in," Piper mumbles when I knock. I open the door and look around her room. A few stuffed animals on the bed. A large jewelry box on her dresser. A checkers board on the desk.

My hands feel funny at my sides. I cross them, fold them, then let them drop back down again. "Hey Piper, I'm just wondering. Are you okay?" I ask.

She gnaws at her cuticle. "I'm fine."

"Okay, second question. Any idea what the task force findings are going to be?"

She squints at me. "I don't think they've finished yet. I did hear one thing . . . don't know if I should tell you about it, though. Can you keep your mouth shut? This isn't something Jimmy or Annie or Theresa should know about."

"Of course," I say, though it bugs me the way she insists everything she tells me is just between us.

She motions for me to move closer. I lean in. She smells of peanut butter. "A knife disappeared the night of the fire."

"A knife? From where?"

"The silhouette board in the cell house kitchen. You know,

that board painted with the shapes of all the knives in black paint so they can tell in an instant if a knife is missing."

"How'd you find out?"

"I was in the window seat of my dad's office. When the drapes are pulled, he doesn't know I'm there. He was talking on the phone to his boss, the head of the Bureau of Prisons."

My head begins to tingle and I start scratching all over. If the cons have a knife, things have really gotten out of hand.

"I heard they're questioning Capone. Think that will come up?"

"Maybe."

"Where are they questioning him and when?"

"This Sunday at Doc Ollie's. They're taking him to Ollie's to pretend to get his knee taken care of. Gonna bandage him up like he's popped out his knee cap or something. It's a ploy so the cons in the cell house won't suspect he's being questioned. I'm pretty sure you can hear what goes on in Ollie's kitchen from the utility shed outside should you be interested."

I look out the window to the cell house across the way. "Think we can get in there without getting caught?"

"We?" she asks.

I shrug. "We're still friends, right?"

She winds her ponytail around her hand. "I wouldn't know."

"Who would know?"

"You, idiot."

"We're friends as far as I'm concerned."

"Then come on," she says, but her voice is flat like it's been run over a few times.

"Now?" I ask.

"We have to scope it out. Why? You got something better to do?"

"No. Of course not," I say.

Doc Ollie is always in his cell house office and his sister works long hours as a nurse in San Francisco, so his house is the quietest one on Officers' Row.

The location of the utility closet on Doc's back porch is perfect, but it's jam-packed full of brooms, buckets, rakes, shovels, a burlap bag full of horse manure, a wheelbarrow, and straw gardening hats.

"What a mess," I say.

"Stinks in here, too."

"You got a plan?"

She nods. "We'll come early on Sunday. Tell everyone Doc Ollie's sister hired us to clean the shed," she says as a gust of wind whips her hair across her face.

"What if Doc Ollie's sister is here?"

"She won't be." Piper pushes her hair out of her eyes. "They wouldn't bring Capone here if she were."

"That's probably right," I say.

"Probably?" she asks.

"Okay, it's exactly right," I tell her, and she smiles.

On the way back to her house, I bring up Annie's concerns.

"Annie's a worrywart," Piper tells me, yanking a vine of tiny yellow flowers from the trellis and ripping off every blossom.

"She says you're . . . acting strangely."

Piper's dark eyes take stock of my face. "I got her a baseball and that's the thanks I get."

"She thinks something is upsetting you, that's all."

Piper snorts. "Annie doesn't know the half of it," she mumbles.

"Do you need help?" I ask as gently as I can.

"Look." She glares at me. "Did I say I wanted to talk to you about this? You're always trying to help everyone, Moose. Do you know how annoying that is? And tell Annie to mind her own business." She turns on her heels and stalks off.

"See you on Sunday," I say.

I don't know if she hears me or not.

19. The Other Jack

Thursday, January 30, and Friday, January 31, 1936

I have just taped two new numbers above my eyebrows, and my mother is beaming at me like I have superhuman powers. Who knows, maybe everything will work out all right. My dad says the task force is going to announce its findings next week. He says we have nothing to worry about, but then, my father is not the worrier in the family. My mother is.

I'm headed upstairs to find Nat when my father comes into the kitchen to pour himself his first cup of coffee of the day. The kitchen in #2E still isn't operational so he has to wait until he comes up here to make coffee. "Look, you two, I want us to put the fire behind us."

"Won't that be easier once the task force report is out?" I ask.

"There's no time like the present to start building trust again," my father says.

"Pretty hard to do when there are so many unanswered questions," my mother says. "I don't know about you, but I can't look Bea in the eye."

"Bea made a mistake, that's all. You've never made a mistake?" my father asks.

"The problem is Bea doesn't think she made a mistake."

"She will. She just doesn't see it yet. Give her time."

My mother is about to object, but before she can say anything, my dad rushes on.

"We can't be holding grudges. This island is too small for that."

My mom sighs, her attention absorbed in her teacup. "I know it," she admits.

"The changes have to start with us."

I nod, waiting for my father to go on.

"Moose. I want you to go out of your way to include Janet Trixle. She sometimes gets left out because—"

"We don't like her parents," I finish for him.

"That's right," my father says. "And Helen, you've been keeping to yourself. I want you to start having coffee at Mrs. Caconi's and playing bridge with the gals again, exchanging recipes, getting your hair done at Bea's, all that hen business.

"And I'm throwing a poker party."

This gets my mother's attention. "A what?"

"A poker party, tomorrow night. You three are going to have to make yourselves scarce."

My mom clenches her jaw. "The medicine is worse than the disease, Cam," she grumbles.

"Now, Helen," my father sighs. He tips his head and raises his eyebrows at her.

"All right, all right, I need to visit Great-Aunt Lydia and Uncle Lester anyway. Moose, could you keep an eye on Natalie during your father's game?" she asks.

"Sure, Mom," I say, like I always do. Who else is going to take care of Natalie?

The next night, my mom leaves on the five o'clock boat. She still hasn't jumped back into the "hen business," as my father calls it, but she gets off the island so my father can have his poker party.

I help my dad drag the card table and the folding chairs from the storage room in 64 up to the Chudleys' house. While I clean the thick layer of dust off the seats, my father puts a pot of unpopped corn on the stove. I can tell from the extra bounce in his step that he's excited about the evening. My father loves to play games. He isn't one to hold a grudge either. He's kind of amazing that way. He's actually looking forward to this.

Soon the Chudley house is filled with the smell of freshly popped corn. I'm hoping my dad will let me stick around. Natalie could go to the Mattamans'. Theresa would watch her. This would work fine.

But as soon as the popcorn and nuts are on the table, Dad tells me it's time to go.

I open my mouth to plead my case, but he's already shaking his head. "Sorry, Moose. This is grown-up stuff."

"I'm not a kid anymore."

"You're not an adult either."

"I'll be quiet. You won't even know I'm here."

"I need you to keep an eye on Natalie."

"Theresa will do that."

He shakes his head.

"Wait . . . Mr. Mattaman and Darby Trixle are playing . . . what about Bo Bomini?"

"You know how the Bominis are about gambling."

"Warden Williams?"

"He said he'd stop by."

"Do you think he will?"

"Nope."

"Won't you need a fourth, then?"

My father smiles. "Nice try. Donny is playing," he says, holding the door open for me and Natalie to leave.

At the Mattamans', Mrs. Mattaman is slamming around the kitchen, mad as a cat in a bathtub. "I don't see why you need to go," she hisses at Mr. Mattaman.

"Let up, honey. It's one evening." Mr. Mattaman looks young for a dad. In civilian clothes, he could pass for eighteen.

"We don't have money to burn, Riv. You know that as well as I do."

"Nobody has money to burn. It's penny-ante."

"Cam's been promoted. Trixle's got Bea's canteen bringing in money, plus he only has the one child."

Riv gives his shoes a last buff. "Don't take it all so seriously, muffin. I'm not going to lose money. This is all in good fun."

She bangs the oven closed.

"Moose, Natalie, good to see you two," Riv says, his eyes on Mrs. Mattaman as he walks out the door.

"Wait!" Mrs. Mattaman trots after him, banana bread in her hand. "You can't go to a party empty-handed," she scolds him.

I can't help smiling at this. Mrs. Mattaman will die with bread in her hands. Her last words will be *Want seconds?*

Mrs. Mattaman's cheeks flush when she comes back inside. "You guys have dinner?"

"Sort of," I say.

She opens the oven, pulls out a pan, and skillfully maneuvers her spatula under two fat manicottis. The smell of her tomato sauce has me salivating. I sink my teeth into the cheesy pasta busting with butter and garlic.

Nat settles down with her favorite Mattaman book. It's full of maps of the states. She traces the routes to the places she knows and adds up the miles so she'll know how far away it is.

Theresa is busy playing school with Rocky as her student. He does nothing she wants with a big grin on his face. "Itty-don," he babbles, which means sit down. Theresa scolds him with her finger. Rocky scolds back as Bea and Janet Trixle knock on the open front door.

I know my father said we have to reach out to everyone, but Bea Trixle? I study the electrical outlet as she walks past me to the kitchen to chat with Mrs. Mattaman.

I would go find Jimmy, but I'm hoping for seconds on the manicotti. For once Mrs. Mattaman doesn't notice my empty plate. She's deep in conversation with Bea.

"Do you want to see?" Mrs. Mattaman asks.

"You bet," Bea says.

Mrs. Mattaman slips past me and comes back a minute later with a white gift box. "Look." She lifts the lid. Inside is a blue dress.

"Oh for goodness' sake, Anna Maria," Bea says. "That's beautiful. Somebody wants to give you a gift, you take it and run. You lost every bit of your baby weight. Who says you shouldn't show off your figure?"

"But who gave it to me, Bea?"

"Does it matter?"

"Yes it matters, and besides that, what will Riv say?"

"It does a man good to think his wife can still turn heads. Besides, you can't give it back. You don't even know who it's from."

The worry crease between Mrs. Mattaman's eyebrows deepens. "You sure you don't know anything about this?" Mrs.

Mattaman asks as Theresa and Janet thunder into the kitchen.

"If I were to guess, I'd say Donny Caconi. He's the only man on the island got that kind of style."

"Donny? Why in heaven's name would he be getting me a gift?"

"You've made him cookies, you know you have."

"I've made everybody on this island cookies, Bea."

Bea laughs. "And what is the problem with having someone appreciative for once? Just enjoy it. He wanted to sign his name, he would have."

Mrs. Mattaman puts the lid back on the box and returns her attention to the dishes. She's forgotten all about me. I'm not getting seconds.

Where is Jimmy, anyway? The door of his and Theresa's room is closed. He's been working on something in there. He won't tell me what it is, and Theresa has been sworn to secrecy, though I'm guessing it has something to do with bottle caps and Donny Caconi. Jimmy didn't even see Donny throw, but he's sure I threw better than Donny.

When I finish eating, I head for Jimmy and Theresa's room and knock on the door. Jimmy answers with the Parcheesi game in his hand. We settle into an epic Parcheesi match, which lasts until ten thirty, when Mrs. Mattaman comes in. "All right you two, time for Moose to head home. It's way past Theresa's bedtime."

It would have been smart to bring our pajamas so we didn't have to go all the way up to the Chudleys' and then back down to #2E again. Living at the Chudleys', everything you need is always somewhere else.

"I'd have you stay the night, but . . ." Mrs. Mattaman's face hardens. "I'd just as soon you broke up their little poker party."

"Sure, Mrs. Mattaman," I say as I collect Nat and we trudge out into the cold misty air. The wind cuts through my sweater. The water laps at the dock, the foghorn booms like God is playing the tuba.

Up top, the Chudleys' house is brightly lit, but when I open the door, the air is stale and smoky. An ashtray overflows with cigarette butts. Empty glasses clutter the side table. Nothing but greasy old maids are left in the popcorn bowl. Mr. Mattaman is rocking back on his chair. Donny has his jacket off, his shirtsleeves rolled up, his feet on a milk crate.

Darby and my dad each have one pile of chips. Mr. Mattaman has a half a pile. Donny's got three huge stacks.

It doesn't take a genius to figure out who is winning.

"FDR is a poker player. Why'd you think he called it the New Deal," Donny says.

"Roosevelt . . . don't let me get started on him. He's a one-term president if I ever saw one," Darby says.

Nat and I wait a full minute but still no one notices us.

"Say hello," Nat blurts out.

My dad's startled smile shines on her. "Hello, sweet pea, you're home early. What time is it, anyway?"

"Ten thirty."

He squints out at the night. "Couldn't be."

Mr. Mattaman glances at his small pile of chips. His face blanches white around the lips. He's clearly lost money. I don't envy him facing Mrs. Mattaman with that information.

Natalie settles in behind my dad, eyeing the cards in his hand. Dad motions with his head like we should get out of here.

"Nat," I whisper. "Come on."

But Nat's feet are planted. Her attention is on the game.

"Nat," I try again, "you'd better check on my toothbrush."

But Natalie's not going anywhere.

Darby Trixle takes a deep drag from his cigarette.

"Nat." I tug on her sleeve. She shakes me off like a mosquito. I look over at my father for help.

Nat's quiet now—she might pitch a fit if we force her to go. My father's eyes take this all in and he nods like we can stay.

They play three hands of something—I don't know what. With each deal Donny Caconi adds more chips to his pile at the expense of Darby. Darby's down to three chips. Mr. Mattaman has held steady. Darby pushes his three last chips into the ante.

"Second black jack," Natalie says. "Second one. *Second* one."

Darby glances up at her, then back down at his hand. "Get her out of here, Cam," he mumbles, the cigarette dangling between his teeth, dropping ash on the table. "She's telling everyone your cards."

"No, she isn't," my dad says.

"Second black jack. Two jacks," Nat repeats.

"You're right, sweet pea . . . there are two black jacks," my dad explains. "A jack of spades and a jack of clubs."

"*Clubs*. Second black jack of *clubs*," Nat shouts.

"Cam, GET HER OUT OF HERE!" Darby bellows. He has a big mouth even without his bullhorn.

Riv Mattaman looks up. His eyes track Nat. He knows what she's capable of. "What's she talking about, Cam?"

"She don't belong here," Darby barks.

Donny smiles kindly at Natalie, but his eyes are blinking twice as fast as normal. "Things never go well when there's a dame in the room."

But then suddenly Donny throwing the bottle caps flashes through my mind. Who would take a kid's money forty-eight hours after his apartment burned down? "You're playing with one deck, right?" I ask.

"Course," Dad says, picking a card out of his hand.

Donny glances at his watch. "Look at the time. Better call it a night." He stands up from the table.

"For Chrissake," Darby snaps. "Can't stop now."

"Two black jack of clubs," Natalie says.

"It's late," Donny says. "We should stop. My mama's gonna be coming up in her nightclothes, wagging her finger at me. '*It's bedtime, Donny.*'" He does a perfect imitation of Mrs. Caconi's old-lady voice. He laughs as his hand creeps to the discard pile, but mine is faster. I curl my fingers around the messy stack and hand it to my dad.

My hands are trembling; sweat drips down my face. This is Donny Caconi. Everybody likes Donny Caconi. The room is so stuffy, I can hardly breathe. "See if there are two jacks of clubs in there," I whisper.

My dad's eyes warn me I've overstepped my place, but he knows Natalie as well as I do.

"One jack of clubs." He flips card after card onto the table, until we see it . . . the grim face of the second jack of clubs. "And here's the second one," my father whispers.

All eyes fly to Donny and his stacks of chips. "Somebody's fixing the game—" Donny announces loudly.

But he doesn't finish the sentence before Darby jumps him from the back, one arm around his neck. Donny shakes him off, sending the table flying and the chairs clanking down. Darby's feet hit the ground, but his left arm shoots back around Donny's neck. "You sneaky piece of crap!" Darby bellows.

"Get Nat out of here," Dad shouts to me as he tries to jump between them.

Natalie rocks from onc foot to the other, her back against the wall.

"Nat!" I call, but she doesn't seem to hear me.

Donny swings, Darby dodges the blow, and it lands solidly in my father's gut.

But Darby still has hold of Donny's neck. His fingers squeeze. Donny chokes. "How dare you cheat me! I should have known," Darby says.

"Let go, you're gonna kill him!" my father shouts.

Darby smacks Donny's ear with his other hand, squeezing his neck, trembling power in his hands. "That'll teach you."

Donny aims a left hook for Darby's face.

Mr. Mattaman dives for Darby. He twists him off Donny. Darby screeches in fury, then kicks Donny in the privates so hard, Donny doubles over in pain.

"Back off!" my father shouts, using Darby's bullhorn.

Riv Mattaman is dragging Trixle off the still doubled-over Donny.

My father takes the bullhorn from his mouth. "You all right, son?" he asks Donny.

Slowly Donny stands upright, his cheek bruised and bloody, his eye already starting to swell, raw red welts along his neck where Darby nearly strangled him.

"Darby?" my father asks.

Darby's lip is bloody. He holds his jaw like it hurts, but his eyes are slits of fury, trained on Donny Caconi.

"Now here's how we're going to play this," my father announces. "Everybody is going to leave this room with the exact money they carried into it. You"—my father points at Donny—"will never play cards on this island again. Do you understand me?"

"Hey," Donny cries, "it wasn't me."

Darby nearly busts out of Mr. Mattaman's hold.

My father's voice is steady. "It was you, son. A queen fell out of your undershirt. I saw it myself, when Darby was on top of you."

Darby snorts, blood spurting out of his nose.

"Darby, go see Doc Ollie. Donny, you're going to have to wait your turn on that. And you can expect the warden to be getting a full report. Your mama is only here because of the warden's kindness . . . don't you know that, son?

Donny's nostrils flare.

"Where's she going to go if he decides he needs that apartment for a guard's family? You keep on with this business, you can bet that's exactly what he'll do. You wanna be responsible for that?"

Donny doesn't answer. His face is blank, like he's still holding cards in his hand. He untangles his coat from the chair turned over on the floor and opens the door. The moon shines on the entryway for one brief second and then he's gone.

My father thumps the table to get Darby's attention. "Don't you go after him, Darby. You hear me?"

But Darby isn't going anywhere. He's looking at Nat, who is crouched in the corner collecting cards from the floor. Darby's feet are parked in front of her, but her eyes are on the cards in her hand.

I hold my breath, willing her to look up. If only she could meet Trixle's gaze right now. If only she could make that connection. *Please, Nat. You saved him a bundle of money. He wants to like you. Can't you pretend to be normal just this once?* But Nat does not look up . . . and the moment passes.

Darby turns to my father. "How'd she know?" he asks.

"You pay attention, don't you, sweet pea?" my father says.

Nat is sorting the cards in her hand, oblivious to us.

"Sure don't look that way," Trixle addresses my father again. "But she must."

Nat starts mumbling. "You pay attention, don't you, sweet pea."

"What'd she say?" Darby asks.

"She said she pays attention," I tell him.

He nods, but still can't bring himself to give her more than a fleeting glance. He continues to direct all of his comments to my dad as if Natalie isn't here at all.

20. Funny Business

Saturday, February 1, 1936

The next morning, I head for the Mattamans'.

"Moose," Mrs. Mattaman says my name like I've been gone for a year. "Where is that sister of yours? She saved us an entire month's pay. I'm gonna get busy here and whip up the best lemon cake she's ever had. That's still her favorite, isn't it?"

"Yeah, thanks, Mrs. Mattaman. She saved Darby money too, but he didn't say boo to her," I tell Mrs. Mattaman.

"Can't say that's a surprise."

"He's always either ignored Natalie or had it in for her. If she would just look him in the eyes, it would make all the difference. I don't understand why she can't fake it."

"One of the things I like about Natalie is she doesn't fake anything, Moose. But I see what you're saying." Mrs. Mattaman pulls out a clean apron, slips it over her head, and ties the sash. "What have you tried?"

"Giving her buttons. Taking them away. Nagging her about not doing funny business. Taping math problems to my forehead. You name it, we've tried it."

She looks at me for a long moment, tapping her pencil against her wooden recipe box. "I'll tell you what, then . . . we got to try something new."

"We've tried it all."

"We got to figure out what makes her tick, that's all. Moose, go get Annie, she's got good ideas. Jimmy, we need that clever mind of yours. Theresa, eat your breakfast. You think better on a full stomach. We're going to figure this out." She shakes her pencil at me. "That's all there is to it."

When I come back with Annie, Mrs. Mattaman scootches over, making room for me on the sofa.

"You want to fill us in on the problem, Moose?" Mrs. Mattaman asks me. "We'll take it from there."

I look around at everyone squeezed together on the Mattamans' worn brown sofa. Theresa, still in her pajamas, Jimmy, his hair wet from the shower, Annie in her new baseball clothes, Baby Rocky with a cake tin on his head.

Mrs. Mattaman finds Rocky's favorite toy hammer and gets him started pounding. "Ang! Ang! Ang!" he babbles.

"Nat has to look us in the eye when she speaks to us. We've tried everything, but nothing has worked," I say as we hear a knock on the door.

Janet presses her nose against the screen. "Hey! What are you doing in there?"

"Come on in and join us, Janet." Mrs. Mattaman nods her head as if to reassure me this will be all right.

"What have you tried?" Annie asks.

I explain about the numbers on my forehead and the Esther P. Marinoff button reward system and Carrie Kelly's focus on funny business.

"Why does she have to learn this? Why can't she do things her own way?" Jimmy asks.

"Because strangers ignore her," I say. "They treat her like she isn't there, like she's not worth anything, because she doesn't look at them."

"Why does everybody have to measure up in the same way?" Jimmy's fingers thread a series of rubber bands. "She's got other strengths."

"That she does. But there are certain things you have to learn to do, like saying *please* and *thank you,*" Mrs. Mattaman tells him. "Part of a mom's job is to help her kids learn the rules so they can be successful out there."

"Did any of the things you've tried work better than the others?" Annie wants to know.

"The numbers didn't work," I say. "She hardly glanced up to read them. The buttons have worked really well for other things, but not for this."

"Let's start off by asking Natalie why she doesn't want to do this," Mrs. Mattaman suggests.

"She won't say," I tell her.

"Maybe she won't, but we gotta try. It's her that has to change. All we can do is help. Go on and get her, Moose."

Back in #2E, Nat is awake but still in her pajamas and my dad is trying to get her up to the Chudleys' for breakfast. He's relieved when I take her off his hands. He doesn't even comment when I march her over to the Mattamans' with her pajamas on. My mom would be furious, but my dad and I think getting Natalie dressed is not worth the trouble. My dad won't brush her hair either. That's a guaranteed fight.

"Natalie," Mrs. Mattaman says, "I heard you were the one who figured out the cheat . . ." Her voice trails off. She eyes Theresa. I don't think she wants her to know that a grown-up was caught cheating. "Uh, you were the one that helped out last night. I was fixing to make you a lemon cake to thank you."

"Lemon cake," Nat whispers.

Now she's talking Nat's language.

"I'm gonna whip it up soon as we finish here. But your brother was telling me you don't like to look at people when you talk to them. That's important, Natalie," Mrs. Mattaman says, "is there some way you can—"

"No," Nat belts out loud and clear.

Mrs. Mattaman smiles. "No, huh?"

"No," Natalie confirms, tasting her lip with her tongue.

"The pixies can help," Janet pipes up. "When I can't do something, they always help me."

"No pixies," Natalie says. She's begun rocking now, sitting on one hand, then the other, trembling with agitation. "Lemon cake."

"Maybe there's something else we could do with numbers?" Jimmy suggests.

"No," Nat shouts. "No Natalie look a person in the eye!"

"Okay, okay." Mrs. Mattaman's palms are up. "We hear you. We want to know why is all."

Nat's shoulders are hunched forward, making her look like a teenaged old lady.

"Natalie, you can tell me," Theresa says. Nat shakes her off, shakes everyone off, like a wet dog shuddering the drops away.

"It's a little too much," Mrs. Mattaman whispers.

"Too much!" Natalie shouts, digging her chest with her chin. "Too much!"

"Nat," I say. "Stop it."

Janet Trixle's eyes are the size of cupcakes. This is just what we need. Janet Trixle reporting this back to her parents.

I pull an afghan from the couch and wrap it around Nat. Having something tight around her usually helps for some reason, but not today. Today she tears the blanket off, angry tears running down her face.

"Lemon cake! Lemon cake!" she demands.

"Calm yourself down, young lady," Mrs. Mattaman tells her. "I'm not making lemon cake for you like this. No misseee."

But Nat is beyond reason. The circuits have popped inside her brain and she can't think anymore.

I hold her in a bear hug, but she thrashes against me, grabbing hold of the doorway as I half carry her out.

"Moose, no!" She bites my arm.

"Ouch!" My hand flies up to slap her. I only barely keep myself from doing it.

I find the blanket again and wrap it around her. This time she accepts the support and allows me to carry her out of there. But I'm so angry, I'm shaking as I lug her back to #2E. I'm not taking her to the Chudleys'. She's too heavy. It's too far.

"I hate you sometimes, Natalie," I practically spit at her, dumping her on the bed in her room. I hold my arm where her teeth punctured the skin.

All I do for her and this is how she treats me?

I'm sick of trying so hard. Why is it always me who tries? Me who worries? Me who does everything?

"It must be fun to be you. You never have to do anything you don't want to do," I say.

Natalie doesn't answer, doesn't move. She's turned into a human stone.

• • •

When my mother gets to #2E, there's no hiding what happened. Nat's pajamas are still on. Her hair is matted and stuck with spit and tears to the side of her face. Her eyes are open. She's perfectly still, like one tiny motion will capsize her world.

My mother takes one look at her and the bottom drops out of her face. "What happened?"

I tell her about how Nat figured out the cheat Donny was pulling with the cards and how Trixle still wouldn't pay attention to her. Then I explain about the meeting at Mrs. Mattaman's.

"Has she even had breakfast?" my mom asks.

"No," I admit.

"You know better than this, Moose."

"She bit me," I say.

My mother groans like she's in pain. "Let me see."

She looks at the bite and then up at me. "Go borrow some Mercurochrome from Anna Maria and put it on that."

I don't move. "We can't parade her problems in front of everyone. We can't have her biting you. With your dad in such a visible position, we have to keep her out of the spotlight now more than ever."

I grind my teeth. "I was just trying to help." I never get credit for anything. It doesn't matter to my mom how embarrassing this was. It doesn't matter that Nat hurt me.

"I know, Moose, but it made everyone more aware of her limitations."

"She isn't invisible. People see her anyway," I snap at her.

"They don't notice until you point it out."

"Sure they do, Mom, they're not blind."

"We can handle this ourselves."

"Since when? We're not handling it. It isn't working. Haven't you noticed?"

"Look at her," my mom says. Natalie is still wrapped in the blanket, still completely shut down. "Is this an improvement?"

"No. Okay . . . this didn't help. And, don't worry, I won't try anything ever again." I stalk to my room, but the door isn't even there. They took it off to repair it. I hunker down in the blankets on the floor where I sleep now. I'm going to forget about the fire. I'm going to forget about everything. I'll just wait around for the task force report like everybody else.

A few minutes later my mom comes in. "I didn't mean that, Moose. I'm sorry. It's just we can't have her throwing tantrums like this. We can't have her biting people. If she behaves that way, she won't be welcome anywhere."

"Yeah, but if we don't try things, how's she ever going to get better?"

Her shoulders sag. She sits down suddenly on a stack of lumber, like her legs have given out on her. "That's the trick, isn't it?" she whispers.

"Let's make it a game." I throw this out weakly. It feels like I have a truck parked on my chest. I can hardly breathe. "She likes games."

"You tried that with the numbers on your forehead," she says, her voice gentle for once.

"A different game, then," I offer.

My mom stares down at her hands. "Fine. But only at home. Not out there."

"She's going to live out there, Mom. You can't keep her in here forever," I whisper.

"Stop." My mother puts her hands over her ears.

I wait until she lets them down again. "She can do this," I say. "She just has to want to. It can't be us wanting for her."

"Don't you see how precarious this is? The Trixles still think she started that fire. The Esther P. Marinoff has her on probation. If she goes back to pitching fits in public, we'll be off this island and out of that school. We'll be nowhere."

"But Dad's a warden now."

"That's not insurance . . . if anything, it makes us more vulnerable. Do you know how badly Darby wants that job?"

"She can do this, Mom."

"It puts too much pressure on her. She bit you!"

"If she can't figure this out, then what, Mom?"

She closes her eyes. I watch the tiny veins in her eyelids pulsing. She doesn't answer me. But she doesn't say no again.

21. Al Capone Eats a Sandwich

Saturday, February 1, and Sunday, February 2, 1936

That evening when my father comes home, my parents go out to watch the sunset, and I get my chance to talk to Nat.

Nat is rolled up in her blanket. "Nat," I whisper. "Every time you look in my eyes, you get a point. The points will add up. You can count them. You can keep track of the score," I say.

She digs her chin into her collarbone and turns her head away from me. But the picture of Darby Trixle ignoring Natalie even after what she did is fresh in my mind. It's late now, but tomorrow I'm going to talk to Annie and Jimmy, Theresa and Piper about this. We have to get everyone to help. We can't do this alone.

When my father is done talking to my mother, I get my turn.

"I can't believe Donny Caconi is a cheater."

He sighs. "I was surprised too. I'm going to have to talk to him."

"Could I come along?"

"Not a chance."

"Why not?"

"You already know the answer to that."

"Is it because I'm thirteen? Because that's not a good reason. I'm old enough. I've earned the right."

He smiles at this. "You have, have you?" he says. "Well, what if I say that I don't want you carrying too much responsibility on your shoulders. What if I say I want you to be a kid while you still can."

"I'd say you're wrong."

"Moose"—he holds my gaze with his—"I'm not wrong."

The next day, on the switchback outside the Chudleys', I see Mrs. Mattaman holding Baby Rocky's hand.

"Bird," she says as she points to a gull. "House." She waves his hand in the direction of the Chudleys'.

"Toody." He points at the ground.

"Ground," she says.

He squats, then bursts up to a standing position. "Toody-toody." He gets all excited now.

Mrs. Mattaman shakes her head like she doesn't understand.

"Toody-toody." He jerks his pointer finger all around.

"Turdy. Bird turdy," I translate.

Mrs. Mattaman laughs. "Leave it to you to figure that out."

"Can I talk to you for a minute, Mrs. Mattaman?" I ask as she chases Rocky, who is trying to catch a seagull, his pudgy arms wide open like he's going to hug it to death.

"Course, Moose," she says, scooping Rocky up, his fist full of feathers.

I tell her about the new idea for helping Natalie. I think she'll be pleased, but she clicks her tongue the way she does when a cake falls. "Did you talk to your mother about this?"

Uh-oh. My mom must have talked to her. She must have chewed her out.

"Yes, ma'am," I say.

She smoothes Rocky's hair out of his face. "I'm afraid I've overstepped my place." She sets Rocky down again. "Maybe I better talk to your mom about this."

"All you have to do is ask Natalie 'What's the count?' She's keeping track herself. Then if she looks at you, you say add one more."

"You're *sure* your mom's okay with this?"

"Yes," I say.

"All righty then," she says. Her voice is reluctant. She twists the ring on her finger.

The clock is ticking. It's almost past time to meet Piper. We have to get in the shed before they show up. Piper is expecting just me, but suddenly I want Annie there, too.

I take off down the switchback to 64 building. I'm panting like a dog when she opens the door of #3H.

"I'm so glad you're not at church." I lean over breathing hard from the run.

She shakes her head. "My mom had a headache."

"C'mon, you should be there when they question Capone."

"Me?"

"You."

"Why?"

"In case I miss something." I look out toward the big hulk of Angel Island. "Because I want you to," I admit.

She wrinkles her nose, takes an uneasy breath. "Okay," she says.

"Thanks," I say. It's just one word, but boy do I mean it right now.

She nods. The corner of her mouth twitches, like it's thinking about smiling. She grabs her coat and follows me.

When we get to Piper's, it's ten minutes after eleven and she's waiting on her step.

"You're late." She looks at me, then at Annie. "What's she doing here?" she asks.

"Another pair of ears," I offer.

"No room in the shed."

"We have to take stuff out anyway," I say.

"You sure you want to do this, Annie? You know you'll get in trouble if you're caught." Piper's eyes are hard.

Annie has a cross on her necklace. She winds the chain around her finger. Her eyes dart toward me. "We have to find out how the fire started," she says.

"We?" Piper asks.

Annie nods.

Piper clamps her mouth shut and hops off the steps.

We follow as she cuts through the side yard between Doc Ollie's home and hers. At the shed, we begin pulling out the brooms, buckets, and ladders and stacking them next to the gardening shack to make space inside. Piper says we should do this out in the open, since our story is that Doc Ollie's sister has given us a job. Two officers walk by on the road. They don't give us a second glance, but Annie's arms are trembling, one hand holds her cross.

When we have enough stuff out of the shed, we slip inside. It's dark. It's stinky, and it's awkward. Being locked in a shed with a girl you once kissed and your best friend who happens to be a girl is not exactly relaxing. I crack open the door, to get a little air.

Annie suggests we play rock, paper, scissors—Alcatraz style. The rock, the newspaper, and the shiv, which is what they call a prisoner-made knife. The shiv stabs the newspaper. The rock smashes the knife. The newspaper covers the rock. I never used to understand that part of the game. I mean, how could a paper be stronger than a rock? But with Bea Trixle threatening to go to the newspaper and what might have happened if she had, it makes perfect sense. One stupid newspaper article could ruin your whole life.

We've just decided they must have changed the schedule and they aren't going to interrogate Al today, when we hear commotion at the front door. I pull the shed door closed and stand in the back with Annie. Piper stands in front. I suck my gut in and rock back into the rakes, so no part of me brushes either of them. But I can't stop thinking about where I am and where they are. At school they say once you've had a crush on someone, it never totally goes away. That explains Piper. I don't want to think about why I also feel weird around Annie.

People are coming into Doc Ollie's kitchen, moving chairs around. From the sound of their voices, I identify Trixle, my dad, and Bo Bomini.

"Uh-oh," Annie whispers. "My father."

"I'll handle the questions, sir," Trixle barks.

"No, you won't," my father informs him in a commanding voice that surprises me.

A chair scrapes the floor. There are more footsteps.

Then I hear Capone. "I'm in the hot seat?"

"That was Capone," I whisper to Piper and Annie. I know what he sounds like because I've met him before.

"Lotta rigmarole for a few questions," Capone says.

"You got a pressing engagement we're keeping you from?" my dad asks.

Capone laughs. "Funny, boss," he says.

"Nothing funny about this, 85," Trixle says in his Double Tough voice.

"You know my memory ain't so good lately," Capone says. "Might want to pour me a high ball—get the gears turning."

"This look like Cook County to you?" Trixle snorts.

"No reason we can't be civilized, now, is there?" Capone mutters.

"Let's get down to business," my father says as I try not to breathe in the manure-smelling air or bump into Piper or Annie. "What do you know about the fire?"

Annie trembles. I have a sudden urge to take her hand, but of course I don't.

"Heard the bell, saw the smoke . . ." Capone says. "That's it."

"What's the word around the cell house about how it started?"

"Dunno."

"Who would know?" my father drills in.

"Can't see how the boys in the big house could have been involved with setting a fire in 64 after lockdown. Just using my noggin for that one," Capone says.

"Who is involved, then?" my father asks.

"Couldn't tell you. Look boys, I keep my nose clean. I'm gonna do my time real nice, then head back home. It isn't me you should be worrying about. Some of them guys up there got a long reach."

"What's that supposed to mean?" Darby asks.

"I ain't speaking Latin, Double Tough. You can figure it out," Capone says.

"I've had enough of your lip." Darby again.

"Take it easy, Darby," my father tells him. "How about the money?"

"What money?" Capone wants to know.

"A lot of money floating around, and gifts. One of your trademarks, isn't it?" my father asks.

Piper moves from one foot to the other, bumping against my arm. I pull away, but she keeps jiggling back and forth, like she can't stop herself.

"I like nice things. Who doesn't?" Capone replies.

"We're talking specifically about gifts," my father says.

Annie gulps. Piper bumps against the shed door.

"Don't know nothing about that," Capone answers.

"It's common knowledge you're the man with the money."

Capone laughs. "Not in here, boss. Course, I have my subscription list. Somebody's a friend, they get my magazines when I'm done. They're not so friendly, I scratch 'em off."

"Nobody cares about your magazines. We want to know where the money is coming from," Trixle demands.

"Beats me," Capone says. "Look, I dunno anything about that fire or any gifts. Got something else I can help you with?"

"You got nothing on the fire?" my father asks.

"Ain't God, you know, fellas. Anything bad happens and you haul *me* in. The sun don't shine . . . you blame me."

"Told you this was a waste of time," Darby snaps. "Cam, can I talk to you outside?"

"Yeah, all right. Bo, keep an eye on him," my father says.

"Don't let him push you around, boss," Capone advises. "You're thc Big Man. Officer Trixle ain't too happy he got passed over. He's not going to stand there and take it."

"Shut your clapper," Trixle explodes.

"C'mon," my dad tells him as Doc Ollie's kitchen door flings open. Their voices are suddenly louder. They're right outside our shed.

Piper breathes in sharply. Annie is so quiet, it's like she's disappeared.

"He's playing with you, Cam," Darby says. "Can't you see it?"

"We all have our own interpretations," my dad tells him.

"It's a big joke the way he calls you boss. You don't hear him pulling that with me. We need to beat the beejeezus out of him. Then maybe we'll get something."

"That's against regs and you know it."

"Regs?" Trixle snorts. "This look like Sunday school to you, Cam?"

"It isn't the Dark Ages either. I'm handling this my way, so behave yourself."

"Behave *myself*?" Trixle's words are full of acid. "Don't let me get—"

"That's right." My father cuts him off. We hear the kitchen door open.

"Lunchtime," Capone announces. "Don't suppose you could make me a sandwich?"

"This ain't no picnic, 85," Darby tells him.

"Man needs nutrition. Memory aid."

"Don't see the harm, Darby. He's gonna miss the cell house gruel," my father says.

"Oh for Chrissake," Darby mutters. "Bo, make him a sandwich."

The icebox opens and closes. Bo seems to be moving around the kitchen. Something clinks, there's the squeak of a jar opening.

"Make you one too, boss? Double Tough ain't hungry, I'm guessing," Capone says.

"You got that right," Darby spits.

"Just being a gentleman is all. World needs better manners," Capone says.

"Spare us," Darby growls.

"What do you know about the point system?" my father asks.

"Don't want nuthin' to do with that," Capone says. "They got *me* on that list same as you and the warden. I'm worth one thing if they spit on me, another if I'm jumped, double if they rub me out. Why would I fund that?"

"Who is behind it, then?"

"Drawing a blank here, boss."

"Seems to me you'll be a whole lot safer if we can find these guys." My father's voice is kind and reasonable.

"I'm not following," Capone says.

"I think you are," my father says.

"Not everybody gets along real good up there," Capone says. "Don't know if you noticed that. Got a few gorillas should be in the zoo. Got 'em on both sides of the bars, if you ask me."

"Which means . . ."

"I said my piece. That's all I know." Capone's voice is softer now.

Darby snorts.

"Knife disappeared from the kitchen," my father says.

"Butcher knife," Capone adds.

"That's right, a butcher knife. What can you tell us about that?" my father asks.

"Got a good system with them silhouettes in the kitchen. You can see real clear when one of them ain't there," Capone says.

"When did it disappear?" Trixle asks.

"I can't say for sure," Capone says.

"Who took it?" my father asks.

"I dunno."

"Who has it?" My father again.

"Dunno that either."

"Why'd they take it?"

"Couldn't tell you."

"C'mon, 85, don't give us the runaround," Darby says.

"I dunno anything about that knife." Capone again.

"You sure?" my father asks.

"Have I always been square with you?"

"No," Darby snorts.

"I ain't asking you, Double Tough."

My father sighs. "All right then, thank you, Al. Doc Ollie will get you fixed up," my father says.

"'Preciate it, boss."

We listen as a chair drags across the floor. The silverware clinks on the plate. The icebox door shuts and then the footsteps fade away.

My neck is sore, my back is cramped, and the horse crap

smell has given me a headache. I push open the shed door and climb out.

Piper shoves past us and takes off down the back stairs we hardly ever use.

Annie watches her, her eyes wide. I know she's surprised they questioned Capone about the gifts. I am too.

"That gift thing . . . Piper's trying to model herself after Capone, that's all," I say.

Annie takes a wobbly breath.

"C'mon. Let's go talk to her," I say as I take off after Piper.

22. The Queen Falls

Sunday, February 2, 1936

I have no idea where Piper is going. I'm guessing maybe the secret passageway, but the passageway door is closed up tight, the screws securely in the hinges.

"The Mattamans'?" Annie suggests. Piper likes Mrs. Mattaman a lot. If she's upset, she may go there.

But the Mattamans aren't back from church yet.

"Wait, is she going to my apartment?" Annie points up to the door that leads to her place.

Annie and I look at each other. "She was just trying to get away from us," I say.

"She doesn't know what to do," Annie says.

When we get to Annie's, Piper is sitting on the doormat. Annie opens her door and Piper charges for the kitchen and pulls out a seat at the Bominis' kitchen table, a card table with an embroidered tablecloth.

Piper looks around suspiciously, the table rocking as she sits down. "No one's here, right?"

"Mom's lying down. She's not feeling well. That's why we missed church. You want something to eat?" Annie asks, opening the bread box and peering inside.

Piper squirms in her chair, like she's ready to jump out of it. "No," she says, but I'm already nodding my head.

Annie stacks store-bought graham crackers on a dish.

Piper unwraps three sticks of gum and stuffs them in her mouth. She dips her hand in her pocket and pulls out a handful of gum and tosses it on the table. Her jaws move like a bone-crushing machine.

"Annie," she says. "Are you going to church tomorrow?"

"Uh-uh. Tuesday nights we go," Annie says.

"Can I come?" Piper asks.

Annie's eyes dart to mine. "Of course," she says.

Piper tracks the look that flies between Annie and me. Her legs are swinging back and forth under the table. "Don't look at me like that. I used to go when I was little."

"I'm glad to have the company," Annie soothes.

Piper chomps her gum. "Annie?" she asks. "Could I spend the night like I used to?"

"Of course."

"Can we go to the Mattamans' for supper and then play Old Maid?" She unwraps another piece of gum and stuffs it in her already packed mouth.

"Whatever you want, Piper," Annie says.

Piper's eyes flick to the Bominis' newspaper, which sits on the side table. She snatches it and heads for the bathroom. The lock turns.

Annie chews at her lip.

"The gift thing could be nothing," I say weakly.

"Then why is she acting like this?"

"I dunno," I mumble. "We have to find out, though.

We can't help her if we don't know what's going on."

Annie's lips bunch to one side. She taps her fist against them, thinking.

She heads for the bathroom door, then knocks gently. "Piper, are you okay?"

No answer.

Annie motions to me. "You try."

I knock on the door. "Piper? Let's talk, okay? Whatever the problem is, I can . . . we can help," I say, but boy does that sound lame. Still nothing.

Annie and I stare at each other.

"We may need an adult," Annie suggests.

"Piper, we're going to go get someone," I call.

This gets a muffled response.

"What?" I ask.

Annie puts her ear to the door. "She says she wants to talk to you."

"Me?" I ask.

I knock on the door, half hoping she'll tell me to go away.

"Come in," she says.

She's sitting on the bathtub rim, her face blotchy like she's been crying, a mess of newspaper by her shoe.

"You don't like me anymore," she says.

Have I caused all this? "Is that what this is about?"

She shakes her head. Her shoulders are hunched over the trash can like she's going to puke.

"You sick?"

"I did something I shouldn't have," she whispers.

"What?"

Piper doesn't answer. Something is really wrong. She never acts like this.

She closes her eyes as tight as they will go, then whispers in a strangled voice, "You have to promise you'll help me."

"Of course I will. Annie and I both will," I say.

"Promise?" She's speaking in a low voice, but the air is full of pressure like before a lightning storm.

"Yes, if I can," I say.

"The money didn't come from my grandma."

My stomach tightens into a ball.

"Where did it come from?" I ask.

"It was magic," she whispers, her voice so low, I can barely hear her.

"Come on, Piper."

"It was." Tears flow down her cheeks. "I put in a dollar and two came back."

"What are you talking about?"

"The laundry. My grandma gave me pin money. I forgot it was in my pocket and I put it in the laundry bag and it went out.

"First thing I did when the laundry came back was check it. I was hoping it would still be there—that it just got washed, but when I dug in the pocket, there were two there."

"Two what?"

"Dollars. I put another dollar in the next week. Two came back just like the last time. And it kept going like that."

"*That's* how you got the money?"

She nods.

"Was there a note? You know, from a con? Or anything else in the pocket?"

"Nope. Just money. Double every time. I didn't want to think about it."

"But you must have thought about it . . ." I say. Piper is a lot of things, but stupid isn't one of them.

She nods, her face buried in her hands.

"Is it okay if Annie comes in?" I ask.

She hesitates for a moment, then nods again. A movement as small as the blink of an eye.

"Annie." I open the door and Annie slips inside.

"Lock it," Piper barks.

Only Mrs. Bomini is out there, but we lock it anyway. "Don't tell her," Piper whispers.

Annie and I look at each other. A piece of the newspaper has been torn out and crumpled up. Annie un-crumples it.

"COUNTERFEIT MONEY FLOWS INTO SAN FRANCISCO," Annie reads.

"Oh no." I shut my eyes.

"What?" Annie whispers.

"You have to go tell your dad right now," I say.

"You said you were going to help me with this," Piper whines. Her face is buried back in her hands. "That's what you said. You help Natalie. You'd help Annie or Jimmy if it were them. Why won't you help me?"

"Annie and Jimmy would never do this and neither would Natalie."

"It was an accident!" she shouts.

"Look. You tell or I will," I say.

"We'll go with you if you want." Annie's voice is gentle. I wonder if she's figured out what the counterfeit money has to do with Piper.

I know what I have to do. I leave the bathroom. My legs

move like I'm outside watching them walk. How could this be happening?

"Moose, c'mon, don't tell," Piper pleads as I open the Bominis' front door, but I keep walking.

I head down to Mrs. Caconi's and pick up the phone. "I need to talk to Warden Flanagan, please."

"Not here. He's doing an airport run picking up some mucky-mucks from Washington. Moose, is that you?"

"Yes, sir," I say. "If my dad isn't here, I need to talk to Warden Williams."

"Ahh, Moose, you know better than that. You can't call a meeting with the warden."

"I have to, sir."

"Is this some kind of a dare you kids are playing?"

"No, sir. It's important."

"You're going to need to tell me more than that."

"It's about his daughter."

"Is Piper injured? Is this an emergency?"

"She's not injured. But it is an emergency. Look, I know this is unusual, but you have to trust me."

I can hear him suck in his breath. He lets it out with a groan. "It better be. That's all I can say. All right, I'll relay the message. We'll see what he says."

I hear the squeak of his swivel chair, the sound of his footsteps, and then the line goes silent. A minute later he's back. "You can speak with Officer Trixle."

"No," I say.

"Excuse me?"

"It can't be Trixle. Look, this is the warden's daughter. We have to talk to *him*."

He grunts. "Moose, you're out of line here."

"I know. You have to trust me. Do it for my dad."

He clears his throat. I think he's going to tell me forget about it, but then he says: "Hold on."

It takes a long time before he comes back. I've begun to scratch everywhere, even my scalp. I've never gotten hives on my scalp before.

When he gets back on the line he says: "Go on up to the warden's house, but this better be important."

The walk up the switchback takes four hundred years. None of us want to face this. But when we finally get to the warden's house, Piper's mom opens the door. She has a glazed look in her eyes. She knows something's up. Her eyes focus on Annie as if Annie's the only one she trusts. Annie looks away.

"Is the warden in his office?" I ask.

Mrs. Williams points to the stairs. "He's waiting for you."

The warden is seated behind his desk. The chain of his pocket watch is twisted, his eyeglasses are crooked. He knows something is very wrong.

The birds tweet outside his window. A buoy dings in the distance. The sky is blue outside, but dark in here. My skin is itching, my legs are shaking. I'm scared out of my mind and it wasn't even me who did it.

"What's going on, Piper?" the warden asks as Piper dissolves into a side chair.

"Moose and Annie and I hid in the shed on Ollie's back porch when Capone was interrogated," Piper mumbles.

"You know better than that," the warden tells her. "You too, Annie."

"When we were there we found out—I found out," Piper whispers, tears sliding down her face.

"You found out what?" he asks.

Piper takes the newspaper out and hands it to the warden. Her hand is shaking hard; the paper flutters.

"COUNTERFEIT MONEY FLOWS INTO SAN FRANCISCO." The warden looks up. "I'm not following this."

No one answers him. He reads the whole article; the room is silent except for the happy-sounding bird tweets outside.

When he's done, he pushes his glasses up on his forehead. "Why is this our concern?" he asks in a terrifyingly quiet voice.

Piper's eyes are glued to her shoes. She takes a wobbly breath and tries to talk, but tears stream down her cheeks. "I found a dollar in my dungarees."

"What?" the warden says.

"The laundry," she whispers. "I left a dollar in the pocket of my dirty dungarees by mistake. When they came back, there were two dollars in the pocket."

The warden's eye is twitching.

"I put in another dollar." Piper's voice is so soft now, you can hardly hear it.

"And two came back?" the warden asks.

She nods. "Then I put in five dollars and ten came back."

"And then what?"

She can't look at him.

"And then what did you do?" the warden's voice booms.

"I spent it."

We listen to the warden's labored breathing.

"How many times did this happen?"

"I dunno."

"Piper!" he thunders.

She looks like she's seen her own death. Her eyes are glazed and her mouth is slack. "Fourteen, maybe more," she whispers.

"Fourteen!"

She nods. "Some weeks I put dollars in more than one pocket."

"It's like gambling," I whisper, not realizing I've said it aloud until the warden responds.

"No gambling involved," he murmurs. "It was a sure thing. Double your money. It never occurred to you to wonder why this was happening?"

"I thought one of the laundry cons, you know, liked me," Piper mumbles, her eyes focused on her shoes. This is the only safe place to look.

"Liked you?"

"Why else would he give me money?" she asks.

Nobody looks at the warden.

"How was I supposed to know it was counterfeit?" Piper's voice again.

"You knew it was wrong," the warden whispers.

"I was going to stop," Piper tells him.

"But you didn't and you guessed it was counterfeit."

"Not at first," she admits. "Then I saw that the Count worked in the laundry. In his file it said he was a counterfeiter."

"Among other things."

"Yes. But I didn't know for sure, until I saw the newspaper. I shopped at the places where they said they found the counterfeit bills."

"Why would the Count give her counterfeit money?" I ask.

"Shhh," Annie says under her breath.

"To get it into circulation," the warden explains. "They got one real dollar and gave back two pieces of worthless paper.

"When did you get your hunch?" the warden asks, spitting the words out like food that's gone bad.

"A couple of weeks ago."

"So you heard them question Capone about the gifts and it made you nervous," the warden asks.

"How could a con make counterfeit money inside of Alcatraz?" I ask.

"Keep control of your mouth, Mr. Flanagan," the warden warns, but then he answers, his voice softening, "Couldn't. He got it from the outside."

"Oh." The word skips across my lips before I can stop it.

The warden's eyes drill into me. "You know something about that?"

"I—I . . . maybe. We were watching the cons on the dock. And it looked as if the Count put something in the rain gutter. So when he left, I checked it."

"And you found . . . ?"

"A note with some numbers on it. I just now figured out what they were. It was a locker number and a combination."

The warden nods. "That's an old trick. He probably has counterfeit bills in a number of lockers in train stations all over. That way he can maintain control. Do you know who picked up the slip of paper?"

"We watched, but we never saw anyone. There was something else too. Donny Caconi beat me at a pitching game. I didn't think he won fair and square, so I looked in his laundry bag to see if there was something—some evidence he cheated." My words come out in a hot rush.

"And?"

"I found forty dollars in Mrs. Caconi's apron. I thought it was real, but maybe it wasn't."

"What did you do with it?"

"I put it back. It wasn't what I was looking for." The warden takes off his glasses and puts his big forehead in his hands. He closes his eyes.

"Did anyone know you had that laundry bag?" he asks.

"Just Natalie. I didn't know it was counterfeit. I didn't know anything. I just thought it was an awful lot of money for Mrs. Caconi to forget in her pocket."

"I didn't know it was counterfeit either," Piper squeaks.

"You." His hands fly up as if to block her. "Do not say one word." His voice trembles.

But Piper can't shut up.

"I thought I was lucky," she mumbles.

"We got a depression going. People don't have a pot to pee in and you're rich as Croesus from *luck*?" The warden's voice is thick.

"All right," he says. "I appreciate you bringing this to my attention. Moose, keep your nose out of cell house business. Annie, you keep him out of trouble. Piper . . ." His eyes move quickly across her as if he has been belted in the gut and can no longer breathe. He puts his head in his hands and closes his eyes.

23. "Am I a Criminal Too?"

Sunday, February 2, 1936

Annie and I head back down to 64. We are both in shock. Our Piper, involved in a counterfeit scheme?

"How could she be that stupid?" Annie says.

"You put in one dollar and two come back. There's something pretty exciting about that."

"Yeah, I know. I could see trying it a second time . . . just to see if it worked. But at what point do you ask yourself what is really going on here? She isn't six years old."

"She used the money to help people. She knows the Mattamans never have enough. Paying Theresa was a good thing and so was that dress Mrs. Mattaman got. That had to have been Piper," I say.

"Yeah, but why do you think she didn't tell anyone?" Annie asks.

"She knew we would tell her to stop," I say.

"I feel bad for her, but I'm kind of mad at her too. She knows better than this," Annie says as we walk down the stairs to the Mattamans'.

Through the window we see Theresa clanking pot lids together, followed by Rocky with a big smile on his face, a pan on his head, and a muffin tin in each hand.

"Piperz otty," Rocky says.

"Naughty," Theresa corrects.

"Otty, otty, otty," Rocky shouts. "Piperz otty!"

"News travels fast," I say.

Theresa sees us and puts her pot lids down. "What happened?" she asks.

When we tell Mrs. Mattaman and Theresa, Theresa's mouth falls open. "I didn't know! Am I a criminal too? Mooooommmeeeeeee!"

"No, sweetie." Mrs. Mattaman smoothes her hair. "We'll get all the money she paid you and we'll pay it back—"

"I don't have it anymore. Not all of it!" Theresa sobs as she runs into her room and comes out with a mason jar, which has a few dollars and some coins.

"I spent some," Theresa cries.

"This isn't your fault, Theresa. You didn't know," Mrs. Mattaman says.

"What's going to happen to Piper?" Annie asks.

"Her dad will take care of it, like he always does," I say.

Mrs. Mattaman shakes her head. "You can't protect a person who breaks laws."

"She has plenty of money," Annie says. "She didn't need to do this."

"That girl has her head screwed on backward," Mrs. Mattaman says. "She had to have known she'd be caught. I hope she learns from this is all I can say."

Part of me is glad Piper finally got caught. As long as I've known her, she's always gotten away with things. I just wish it was for something little.

Thank goodness she didn't pull me into this scheme. I've

been a sucker for Piper plenty of times. My head hurts just thinking about it. I need fresh air.

"You want to play ball?" I ask Annie.

"Now?" Annie asks like I've suggested swimming with sharks.

"Why not?"

"Probably the best thing for you," Mrs. Mattaman agrees.

Annie heads out to get her baseball gear with me on her heels.

I look out at the sun, low on the water. "C'mon, let's go," I say. "We don't have much baseball time left."

But even as we walk up to the parade grounds, more pieces start to fall into place. "Piper pretended she got a gift from a secret admirer. But I don't think there was a secret admirer."

Annie nods. "She wanted to make you jealous."

"I guess so. The thing that's strange is she never seemed to care if I was her boyfriend or not."

"Until you weren't," Annie offers. "I was always supposed to be her best friend. I could never have another best friend even though she really didn't want to spend time with me."

"I guess she just wanted you as a pinch hitter—always ready just in case," I say.

"Yeah, maybe. I'll pitch," Annie says. "You hit."

She winds one up and sends a soft pitch my way. My timing is off. I can't hit the ball to save my life.

"Shape up, Moose," Annie barks.

I set my bat down. "Do you still like her?" I ask.

Annie sighs. "Golly, I don't know. I suppose I like her sometimes. What about you?" Annie's face flushes like she wishes she hadn't asked this.

"Not as a girlfriend," I say. "I can't trust her, but I feel like I should have . . . I don't know, stopped her from doing this."

"How could you stop her when you didn't know what she was doing?"

"I couldn't," I agree. The gulls are closer now. They know we aren't playing ball anymore.

"Moose, you can't be responsible for everyone."

"I guess not."

"Promise me you'll never do anything stupid like that," she says.

"I don't need to promise, I never would."

"Sometimes you get a little, I don't know . . . desperate about Natalie," Annie observes.

"You try being Natalie's brother," I say.

"It must be hard," Annie concedes, her brow furrowed. "But if I were Natalie, you're the guy I'd want for my brother."

"Thanks," I say.

"You're welcome." She tries to shrug this off, but her face is red again.

We start tossing the baseball back and forth, but neither of us seems to be able to concentrate. The ball has become just a round object. Not everything it usually is to me.

We sit down on the hill that faces San Francisco to watch the sun set. The sky is pink, the water orange. The windows of the buildings in the city glint like tiny mirrors in the setting sun.

"Annie," I say. "You look different."

"No, I don't," she mumbles.

Now my face is flushed too. And then out of nowhere, I'm leaning toward Annie. I'm not thinking. I'm too tired and worn out to think. I'm inches away from her now. She smells like baby powder and mint.

She freezes. Her face is stiff, her eyes too large. And then the tiny Annie smile flashes across her lips and I know she wants to kiss me too.

Her lips feel springy, her breath smells like spearmint, her hair is as soft as puppy fur. Who knew kissing Annie Bomini would feel so nice? We sit there for a minute, my arm warm against hers. The sun is down now, but it isn't night yet. One time is gone and the other has not yet begun.

We get up and start walking back to 64. "Forget we did that," I say.

"I've already forgotten," she says.

But I'm still holding her hand and I won't let go.

24. State Problem

Saturday, February 8, 1936

A week later, I still haven't made sense of the changes happening all around me. I mean, I kissed Annie Bomini! How did that happen? And the weirdest thing about it is . . . I wouldn't mind doing it again. It's different when you kiss someone you really care about. It's like when you're there in person at a baseball game instead of just hearing it on the radio.

Jimmy and me are outside the canteen when we hear the task force report is finally released. "It's Donny Caconi." Annie runs down the steps to tell us.

"I knew all along," Bea Trixle informs Annie as she puts the empty soda bottles in the wood tray.

I'm eating an apple and it's all I can do to keep from spitting it out. "How could she have forgotten she blamed Natalie?" I whisper to Jimmy.

"She remembers what she wants to remember," Jimmy tells me.

"Did she give you your job back?"

"Yep, I start tomorrow. Brought the pie up this morning."

"They think Donny was the guy who brought in the counterfeit money for the Count too," Annie says.

"That's not a surprise," I say.

"Annie told me you figured out the note in the downspout was the locker number and combination. That was smart, Moose," Jimmy says.

"I didn't tell you guys about the money I found in Mrs. Caconi's pocket, though."

"What were you doing looking in Mrs. Caconi's pocket?" Jimmy asks.

My face gets hot. I can't look at either one of them. "I wondered if Donny rigged the bottle cap contest. I was looking to see if I could find any, you know, evidence," I mumble, hoping they won't think I have a fat head.

"He rigged it," Jimmy says. "The question is why?"

"Yeah, why cheat a bunch of kids out of a dollar and change," I ask.

"He needed money," Annie says. "He owes a bunch of money to a loan shark. My dad says he was in way over his head. And when you owe money to a loan shark, they'll beat you up if you don't pay it back."

"He needed big money. That was little money," Jimmy says.

"Not to me," I say.

"Could be he just wanted to practice on us," Jimmy says.

"Know what else I heard?" Annie says. "The Count picked Piper as the target for the counterfeiting because she's the warden's daughter."

"Well, she also left the dollar in her pocket. Maybe that gave him the idea."

"Good point," Jimmy says.

"But wait, why would Donny set fire to our place? That's the part I don't get."

"Me neither," Jimmy agrees.

"Did he think there was money at our house?"

"Must have."

"Maybe he stole it and then he burned the house so nobody would know."

In the afternoon, I wait for Annie on the balcony. My mom and Natalie are at the swing set. Dad is down at the dock. He's talking to Officer Trixle, who is directing the cons as they unload bags of laundry from the Angel Island ferry and put them in the back of the truck to shuttle up the hill to the laundry building. Annie is taking a long time to come out. Her mom says she'll just be a minute, but it is the world's longest minute. I toss the ball low. If it hits the balcony ceiling, Darby will hear and then he'll chew me out.

Down below, the dock cons have filled the back of the truck, and Darby is barking directions. Mr. Mattaman is behind the wheel. Two of the cons hop in the truck. The truck door slams shut and Mr. Mattaman guns forward.

Indiana and Lizard are standing around down at the dock, like always. The Count isn't around. They probably tossed him in the Hole. I don't think there's even toilet paper in the Hole. Bet he'll wish he had his counterfeit money then.

The bell rings and all the cons form a line. "One, two, three . . ." They count off for Darby. Darby writes the count on his clipboard and saunters over to the guard tower. He stuffs a cigarette in his mouth, then yanks the guy-wire pulley—the signal for the dock tower guard to send down the clip. I toss my ball a little too hard and it bonks the ceiling. Luckily, Darby doesn't hear it.

"Annie?" I call, but I don't want to knock on her door and

get Mrs. Bomini, again. Talking to Mrs. Bomini is like eating too many sugar donuts. Every other word is *dearie* or *sweetie* or *honey love*.

My eyes flicker back down to the dock. Lizard moves his head toward Indiana like he's telling him something. I'm still tossing the ball, still catching it, but I'm thinking about the cons' points game.

Indiana—the guy with no eyebrows—and Lizard, who should probably be named Cockroach now, are hanging back. With Darby looking the other way they come together like schoolgirl friends. But they're moving differently. Not relaxed and easy, but short and jerky. My baseball is moving through the air in slow motion. I catch it solidly as words float through my head.

Indiana. That's his name, but it's a state. *State problem*. That was the note on my homework. I thought it was about the thesis. Why would Capone care about my thesis?

Then I see it. A flicker of silver glistens. My throat closes. I can't breathe.

"Dad." I gasp for air, but my lungs are jammed flat. I feel the roundness of the ball in my glove. "Dad," I manage to whisper, the fear crushing my chest.

The glint of the knife flashes in Indiana's hand. The ball is in my palm. I aim for the knife, aim with everything I've got. My fingers release, the ball slices through the air. It hits Indiana's head as his knife hand thrusts toward my dad.

The ball slams his ear. His knife hand jerks back.

My voice busts out of my chest. "Dad!" I shout. But it's too late.

My father is down.

Time has stopped. I'm half running, half flying. I can't feel my feet, but I hear the pounding sound of my footsteps. Down the stairs, skipping steps, sailing past the landing. *Please, please let him be all right.* I breathe in small panicky bursts. The dock tower guard trains his Browning automatic on Indiana, who dives into the bay. The gunfire cracks, the water splatters.

"Dad!" I cry. Mr. Mattaman and another guard are bending over him now. Holding him up. His skin is the color of onions, transparent and white.

He's fine. He's fine. He's fine. And then I see the blood.

They rip off his jacket. His shirt has a dark red splotch. The stain is spreading.

Word has gone up for Doc Ollie. He is on the way.

"Moose, are you okay?" somebody asks. I'm shaking hard, my teeth are chattering.

"Where is Doc Ollie?" someone else wants to know.

What is taking Ollie so long? My face is sweating. My skin is hot, then cold as stone. I can't tell if one minute has passed or twenty.

My mother has her arms around my father. Mrs. Mattaman pulls me away. But I twist out of her arms. "Dad! Dad!"

"It's going to be okay, Moose," Mrs. Mattaman keeps saying over and over again, but each word is an envelope with nothing inside.

25. In Charge of Everything

Saturday, February 8, 1936

I can't get the picture of my dad out of my head. His closed eyes, his purple eyelids, the red stain the size of a handprint on his shirt. My mom, Doc Ollie, Bo Bomini, and Mr. Mattaman took him to the city on the Coast Guard cutter. The ferry was at Fort Mason. The Coast Guard cutter was faster.

I wanted to go with him, but Doc Ollie said no. "They won't let you in the hospital. You have to be sixteen," he said.

I'm old enough to see my father get stabbed, but too young to go to the hospital with him. This makes no sense.

Mrs. Bomini is out sweeping the balcony. She shakes her head when she sees me. "We're praying for you, honey. Your daddy is the cat's pajamas and we all know it."

I head up the hill to Piper's. When she opens the door, I stare at her, speechless.

She nods, as if she's expecting me. "Come on," she says. I follow her to the kitchen.

"What do they know?" I ask.

"His name is Lonnie McCrae and he's from Kokomo, Indiana. They started calling him Indiana because at his last prison, there were two Lonnies. The name stuck."

I grind my toe into the rug. "What else do you know?"

"He's in for armed robbery. Sent to reform school when he was thirteen."

"Thirteen. That's how old we are."

She nods, her face a little paler. She could have been sent to reform school too. If she'd been anyone else's daughter, she probably would have been.

"Been in prison off and on since then. He's twenty-nine today."

"He tried to kill my dad on his birthday?"

"Yes," she says.

My head gets woozy. I start sweating all over. My feet pound into Piper's bathroom. I hold the cold toilet bowl while my breakfast comes up in a big pink raspberry jam mess. I wash my face, scrub so hard, the skin is raw, but no amount of soap can make me feel okay again.

Back in her kitchen, Piper watches me, her brown eyes serious.

But I can't sit still. I have to leave. Piper calls to me, but I'm already out the door, half running down the switchback around the bend by the morgue when I come face-to-face with Warden Williams.

"Mr. Williams, sir, why'd they want to hurt my dad? Was it really for a game?"

He nods, his voice unusually gentle. "Indiana wanted a feather in his cap. That's how he thought he'd get it."

"That's sick."

He motions to the cell house. "Some of the men in there are broken in ways that can't be fixed."

"All for a game?"

"A couple of gangs each put a man up. That's always the way it is. But your dad's gonna be all right. He's tougher than he looks. Can't think of anyone I'd rather have my back. Can you?"

"No, sir."

"Hold a good thought, Moose. We'll get through this, you and I."

I head down to the water. It's raining now . . . water hits the top of my head and drips off my nose. I sit with my legs hanging over the dock watching the gray water. The birds are hunkered down, the distant rush of the rain comes through the gutters in 64. The bay laps against the rocks, hollow sounding under the wooden planks.

I don't see Jimmy and Mrs. Mattaman coming, but suddenly they are there. Mrs. Mattaman shivers under a blue umbrella. Jimmy's curly hair is so wet, it hangs straight. "Moose, come on up with us."

I shake my head.

"It breaks my heart to see you sitting out here," Mrs. Mattaman says.

I watch the birds ride the choppy waves, a new shower of rain battering them down.

Mrs. Mattaman puts her short arm around me awkwardly. She is warm and dry, which makes me realize how sopping wet I am. "No rhyme or reason to it," she says. "There's no point in looking for one."

"I saw it. And I opened my mouth and I tried to yell. But I couldn't."

"Moose, now you listen to me. You threw that ball and you hit Indiana. He would have killed your daddy for sure if not for you. But he didn't. And now your father has a fighting chance."

"It's because we spent so long watching the cons. You knew how to read them," Jimmy says.

"No," I whisper. "I didn't figure it out."

"Figure what out?" Jimmy asks.

"Capone warned me."

"You're talking nonsense," Mrs. Mattaman says.

"Capone wrote on my homework *state problem.* Indiana is a state." I am out of breath. I shouldn't be, but I'm so upset, I can't even breathe the right way.

"Nobody in his right mind could have figured that out. Especially given all the craziness gone on here in the last month. How were you supposed to know what that meant? Jimmy, did you know anything about this?"

Jim shakes his head.

"But don't you see? I'm supposed to keep track," I say.

"Of what?" Mrs. Mattaman asks.

"Of everything," I tell her. "Natalie needs my help, and my dad, he never thinks anything bad will happen. Maybe if I'd been a better friend to Piper, she wouldn't have gotten in trouble. I messed up."

"Oh for goodness' sake, you listen to me. You don't have that much power, Moose." She looks at me with her kind brown eyes.

"What happens is in God's hands. Not yours. We're all praying. Every one of us. Everybody loves your father. And he's gonna pull through because your daddy's a fighter. And you? You should feel proud of yourself for thinking quick with that noggin of yours and throwing that ball with your beautiful throwing arm, do you hear me?"

"But I could have yelled," I shout.

"You did yell," Jimmy points out.

"How do you know?"

"I heard you."

"Not soon enough. Not loud enough," I say.

The wind whistles up under Mrs. Mattaman's umbrella, lifting it almost out of her hands.

"Oh fiddlesticks, Moose—"

"Wait, Mom, let's test it out," Jimmy says. "Where were you when you threw the ball?" he asks.

"On the balcony outside the door to Annie's," I say.

"You go to the spot where your father was standing. I'll run up and I'll shout like you did. And then you'll know if your father could have heard or not," Jimmy says.

He doesn't stop to ask if I think this is a good idea. He's already running up the steps to the door to Annie's third-floor apartment, #3H. Mrs. Mattaman stays down with me.

Jimmy waves when he's on the balcony. Mrs. Mattaman tilts her umbrella to the side and jiggles it over her head and Jimmy shouts.

I can see his mouth moving, but I can't hear what he's saying. The rain and the water rushing through the downspouts fill my ears. Mrs. Mattaman turns to me. "You hear that?" she asks.

"No, but it wasn't raining."

"Grant you that, but even so . . . you're listening for it. You're trying to hear it. Your father was not."

I nod. One tiny corner of the weight on my chest lifts.

"If I'd been smarter and figured it all out sooner . . ."

"What you told me didn't add up to diddly-squat."

"But it did."

"Oh flibbertigibbets, Moose." She rolls her eyes. "We'll

report that you think Capone scribbled a note on your homework. Of course we will, but honey, any one of those cons up there is a murderer. Every five minutes a new plan is hatched. For escape, for stabbing a warden, and God knows what else. These men are dangerous . . . surely this isn't news to you."

She takes my chin in her hand and looks deeply into my eyes. "You did your best with that whole big heart of yours and that's all any of us can do."

Jimmy is back down now. "You didn't hear, did you?" He slicks his wet hair back.

"No," I admit.

"I didn't think so," he says.

"There, so now we know. Now, we got other fish to fry." Mrs. Mattaman wiggles her umbrella at me. "I need you to go talk to Natalie. Natalie loves her daddy as much as you do. And she's awful confused right now. I tried to tell her what was happening, but she curled up and hasn't moved since.

"Theresa, bless her heart, has been trying to see to her, but she needs you."

"Yes, ma'am," I say.

"All right then. You march right on up there and go talk to your sister. Jimmy, you go on up and get on dry clothes."

Mrs. Mattaman is right about most things. But wrong about Al Capone. He was trying to warn me.

Still, if Capone really wanted to help, he could have told my dad that day in Doc Ollie's kitchen. He could have prevented this, but he wasn't willing to stick his neck out. Al Capone isn't as brave as people think he is. My dad has more courage than he does.

26. Nat's Turn

Saturday, February 8, 1936

When I get up to Mrs. Mattaman's, Natalie is lying on Theresa's bed with her face down, her legs and her arms tucked under her. She's so quiet, it doesn't look like she's breathing.

"Natalie," I whisper, "do you understand what's going on?"

She doesn't answer but she knows something, or she wouldn't be frozen like this on Theresa's bed.

Usually it ticks me off when she does this, but not today. Today I wish I could shut the world out just like she does.

"Natalie . . ." My voice trails off.

I listen to the sounds of the Mattamans' apartment. Theresa and Jimmy's bottle cap curtain tinkles in the breeze. Baby Rocky babbles to himself. The teakettle whistles, the icebox opens and closes.

I put my hand on Nat's arm, but her skin twitches away. "Daddy got hurt, Natalie."

Natalie rolls side to side as if to burrow herself more deeply into Theresa's mattress.

"Mommy and Doc Ollie took him to the hospital."

"Hospital," she echoes.

"You know what that is."

"Where hurt people get better," she whispers, her face toward the wall.

My eyes focus on the snarl of her hair. What do I say now?

Nat mumbles something I don't catch.

"What?" I ask.

"Have to see Daddy," she says, louder this time.

"You can't," I tell her. "Like I said, he's in the hospital."

"Visit him, visit." She digs her chin into her collarbone.

"You have to be sixteen or they won't let you in the hospital," I tell her.

Nat sits up. She presses her hand against her chest. "Natalie is. *I* am sixteen."

"Yeah, but I can't go, and you can't go by yourself."

"I AM SIXTEEN," Nat says, like maybe I've lost my hearing. "I can go in by myself. I am the warden's daughter."

Don't be ridiculous, I'm about to say. But slowly Natalie's words seep into my brain. *I am sixteen. I can go in by myself.*

I'm not old enough, but she is.

Still, I can't let her do that. My mother would kill me.

Then I remember what Mrs. Kelly said about my parents being older. About how I will be taking care of Natalie someday. Natalie's got to keep trying things, or we'll never know what she's capable of. It's like in my homework report—after FDR got polio, his mom wanted him to retire and sit around for the rest of his life.

He wouldn't be our president if he'd done what his mother said. He'd be a crippled man sitting all by himself somewhere.

It's early afternoon, but it's so stormy and dark outside, the light is on in the hall. I stare stupidly at the pattern it creates on the wall. "Okay. Let's do it."

Nat trembles, but she doesn't get up.

"Nat?" I whisper.

Her trembling gets worse; she's shaking now like she's freezing. And then without a word, she gets up and goes in the bathroom.

When she comes out, she has Theresa's hairbrush. She heads for the kitchen, where she hands it to Mrs. Mattaman and stands quietly, with her back to Mrs. Mattaman, waiting.

Mrs. Mattaman takes the cue and gently begins to brush her way through Nat's tangled hair. "What's up?" she asks me.

"We're going to the hospital," I say.

"You aren't old enough."

"No, but Natalie is."

I can almost see the news travel through the presses in Mrs. Mattaman's brain.

"Moose, honey—" She's going to tell me no. Her mouth opens, then closes again. She works through Natalie's tangles as Nat stands patiently.

Section by section, she brushes her hair until every bit of it hangs straight. Then she takes a rubber band and puts Nat's hair in a ponytail and ties it with a ribbon.

"Now let's have a look." Mrs. Mattaman turns Natalie around.

"You need a clean blouse. Let me see what I have." She comes back with a white button-down shirt and a blue sweater that matches Nat's skirt. My mother would never suggest this. It's not the kind of thing Natalie wears. The stiff fabric will drive her crazy, but Natalie takes it and right there in the middle of the Mattamans' living room, begins to undress.

"Not here, Nat." Mrs. Mattaman gently pushes her into the bathroom and shuts the door.

Nat's in there a long time, but just as I get ready to knock, she opens the door.

When she walks out, she looks as grown-up as a teacher in Mrs. Mattaman's sweater, with the ribbon and too-high ponytail.

I worry she'll throw a fit in these unfamiliar clothes, but something about the still shaky way she's walking tells me how hard she's trying.

Mrs. Mattaman sees my concern. She bites her lip and crosses her arms in front of herself, but she does not tell me we can't go.

Nat's all ready now. Mrs. Mattaman hands us umbrellas and gives us detailed instructions on how to get to the hospital. Nat takes her umbrella into the bathroom and begins flushing the toilet over and over.

"Nat," I call through the door. "We have to go."

She can't manage this. It's too hard, I think, but a minute later she's out of the bathroom, walking through the Mattamans' front door.

"Good luck," Mrs. Mattaman whispers as I scoot after Natalie.

But Nat doesn't walk down to the ferry. She heads for #2E.

"You need something, Nat?"

She doesn't answer but goes straight to her room, then comes out again. I'm expecting her to be carrying her button box, but she doesn't have it.

"What did you get?" I ask as she brushes past me, headed down to the dock.

She doesn't answer.

The ferry trip across the water to San Francisco goes smoothly. Nat doesn't feed the birds like she usually does. She doesn't count the boats on the bay either. She just sits quietly, her eyes on her lap. Even finding the address is no problem with Mrs. Mattaman's careful instructions. But when I see the hospital ahead, my feet slow down.

The place is an enormous building with fancy brickwork and a grand entrance. How can I send Nat in there all by herself? What was I thinking?

"You know, it's probably better if I go with you, Nat," I say.

"Moose is thirteen," Nat mutters.

"Yeah, I know, but . . ."

"I am sixteen." She points to her chest.

But what if this doesn't work? What if she pitches a fit? My mom doesn't need this on top of what's happening with my dad.

"I'm big for my age. I can pass for sixteen," I tell her.

"Moose is thirteen," Nat says. "Thirteen, thirteen."

I have to let her do this. I have to let her try. This is her fight, not mine. "Okay," I tell Natalie. "Go up to the lady in the front reception desk and ask for Dad's room number. You'll have to look in her eye and ask. Say: 'I am Cam Flanagan's daughter. I'm here to visit him. May I have his room number, please?'"

"I am Cam Flanagan's daughter. I'm here to visit him. May I have his room number, please?" Nat echoes.

Nat will have no trouble finding the room number. The hard part is looking normal to the lady.

"Remember, Nat, look the lady in the eyes. No funny business."

"Look the lady in the eyes. No funny business," Nat repeats. "Three."

The game isn't working very well. I wonder if she has even made eye contact twice.

"She's not going to know our game, Nat. You'll have to count to yourself."

"Count to yourself." She rocks wildly from side to side.

Natalie digs a quick jab of her chin on her shoulder. She shakes her head like she's getting snow out of her hair. "No funny business. Count to yourself," she mutters.

"Go on. You can do it."

Nat's chin starts to dip down again, but she stops herself midway. She walks forward flat-footed, as if every part of her foot must make contact with the ground. I'm holding my breath watching her push through the door and walk up to the reception desk.

Will she stop at the counter? Did I tell her not to repeat what the lady says? I never realized how many millions of things you have to do to look normal. How confusing it must be to figure it out.

A man is in line ahead of her. She waits her turn. I see the angle of Nat's face. Her head is up. It's Nat's turn now. She walks forward and begins talking to the gray-haired lady behind the desk.

The gray-haired lady nods. She checks her clipboard, then points Natalie down the corridor.

Natalie hesitates a moment, not sure if she's missed something. The gray-haired lady squints at her.

Does she suspect something isn't right with Natalie?

Maybe. But then Nat moves on and the next person in line goes up to the counter. Nat keeps walking down the hall. She turns a corner and disappears.

27. EYES

Saturday, February 8, 1936

Standing outside the hospital is torture. Anything could be happening in there. I realize too late that I should have had Natalie come back and tell me the room number. Then I could walk on by when the gray-haired lady wasn't looking. If I go and ask now, I'm afraid she'll stop me. I'm tall, but I can't pass for sixteen. If I were to get by the reception lady, I might be able to slip inside. I'm just thinking about this, when I see my mom walking through the lobby and out the front door, her eyes bleary, her face puffy and red.

"Mom!" I pounce on her. "How is he?"

"Moose?" She wraps her arms around me. "He's better, honey," she whispers in my ear. "The doctor said he was too tough to die."

The news hits me hard. It takes me a full minute before I can even take in what she said. And then slowly the relief seeps in. My legs wobble from the sheer force of it. My mom is still holding on to me as if she can't let go.

"Mom," I whisper, "Natalie's up there."

My mom blinks. "Up where?" she asks.

"Don't get mad. She went in by herself."

"No." She shakes her head hard as if it hasn't happened yet, and she's telling me no.

"It's already done. She's in there," I whisper. "She asked for help at the counter and then she went up."

"You sent her in there alone."

"Yeah," I say, "I did."

"I didn't have enough problems?" she asks as she whirls me by the information desk. The gray-haired lady stands up. She opens her mouth to object. She can tell I'm not sixteen. But my mom yanks me up the stairs.

The gray-haired woman follows us, waving her cane. "Stop! No children in the hospital," she commands.

A wizened old man in a doctor's tunic with a stethoscope around his neck sees us coming up.

"Doctor! Stop them," the gray-haired lady shouts.

The doctor gives us an elfin smile. "Stupid rule," he mutters.

"What? Mrs. Dubussy? What? You know I'm hard of hearing. What do you need?" He winks at us.

My mom and I keep going. When we get to my dad's room, there is Natalie sitting by his bed. She has his toothpick box out and she's counting all the toothpicks, placing them carefully around one familiar four-hole button.

"You brought it for Dad," I say.

"Brought it for Dad," she whispers. "It's special."

"Natalie," my mom sighs.

"I am sixteen now," Natalie says, her words like a wall keeping my mom at bay.

"Yes," my mom tells her, a sob hiccupping out of her throat. She dabs at her eyes, trying to recover. "You are."

Nat nods, but keeps counting toothpicks.

"Good job, Nat," I tell her.

"Good job, Nat," she says.

My father is asleep and my mother won't let us wake him. He looks like crap, his cheeks sunken in, his skin the color of fog. But I have never been so happy to see anyone. I don't want to leave here ever. I flat out refuse when my mother tries to hustle us from the room.

"Your dad needs his rest," she says.

"We're just sitting here," I plead, but she'll have none of it.

She lets us each kiss him and then she bustles us out the door.

The pounding inside my head is easing. I didn't even realize my head hurt so much, until now when it's going away. My father is going to be fine.

I don't know if Natalie feels better or not, but I sure do. "Four, four, four," she mutters under her breath.

"Four," I tell her proudly.

Each time we pass someone, she fixes her green eyes on them and calls out a new number. We're getting some strange looks, but for once I don't care.

28. The Pixies' Secret

Wednesday, February 19, and Saturday, February 22, 1936

Dad comes home from the hospital after eleven days. His pants and shirt hang on him like he's wearing another man's clothing and he walks as if he has to think about each step. I wonder how long it will be until he is completely well.

I'm hoping we don't leave Alcatraz. Strange as this may seem, it's my home now. Still, I know my dad's days as a warden are over. I'm not sure I'll be able to stand it if the warden promotes Trixle, though. I'd rather clean all seven hundred toilets on this island than have Trixle be the warden.

A few days later, I see my father with his officer's cap. He's flicking the blood off the badge and scrubbing the bloodstain from the fabric with a soapy rag. "What're you doing?" I ask.

"Got to get my uniform shipshape," he tells me.

"Why?"

"I'm back part-time starting next week."

"Doing what?" I ask.

"My job."

"Associate warden?"

"Course." He looks up at me. "What did you think?"

"I thought you might go back to being the electrician."

He snorts. "Do I look like a quitter?"

"No. But, Dad . . ."

He scrubs harder. "If Trixle had been the associate warden, he'd have been worth five thousand points dead too, you know. It wasn't personal."

I don't want to come out and say I don't think Indiana would have tried to hurt Darby Trixle, so I keep my trap closed.

"Dad?" I ask.

He sticks a toothpick in his mouth and chomps down hard. "I'm listening."

"The night of the fire . . ."

"Uh-huh."

"I did something I wasn't supposed to do."

"Which was?"

"I fell asleep."

His hand stops moving. He looks up at me. I hold my breath. "What the devil, Moose?" He takes the toothpick out of his mouth. "It never occurred to me you'd wait up."

"It didn't?"

"Course not." He dips his rag into a jar of polish. "We weren't staying up with her before the fire either. The whole world doesn't rest on your shoulders, buddy."

I close my eyes and let my head fall back. When I open them again, my father is watching me. "You know, I was glad to hear you let Natalie go into the hospital on her own. That was a big step for you."

"For *me*?"

He nods. "It's not easy being in charge, Moose . . . you think I don't know that? Harder to be Natalie's brother than it is to be a warden. And being a warden is no picnic.

"People are responsible for themselves. All you can do is

try to inspire each person to be his best self. You did that with Natalie. You let her do what she needed to do. Your mom could never have done that. You know that, don't you?"

I look into my dad's deep brown eyes. It never occurred to me he understood what I was going through. I wish I'd talked to him about falling asleep the night of the fire a long time ago.

That's what I'm thinking when I hear a kid-size knock on the door. I know it's not Theresa, because she would have already come inside.

"Door's open," I shout, heading out of my parents' room.

"Hi." Janet waves with one hand up high near her face. She carries her new pixie house—a shoe box decorated with cut-out paper—into the kitchen and sets it on the table.

"Hi," I say.

Janet stares at me like she's expecting me to do the talking.

"Did you want something?" I ask.

She nods. "The pixies know something they aren't supposed to know," she announces.

"That's nice," I say.

She crosses her thin arms. "They want to tell you what it is."

"Uh-huh." I flip open the bread box door to see if there is anything decent to eat.

"But the pixies will never say this again."

"Umm," I mumble. I've found a piece of Natalie's lemon cake and I'm dividing it into three tiny slivers. One for me, one for Janet, and one for Natalie.

"The pixies know who set the fire."

I look over at Janet. "Donny Caconi set the fire," I say.

Janet nods.

"The pixies said you have to promise never to tell."

I put the lemon cake slices each on a plate. "Everybody knows it was Donny."

"That's not what you have to promise," Janet tells me.

"I promise," I mumble, handing her a piece of cake. I have no idea what she's talking about.

Janet takes the top off the shoe box and begins unloading her pixie stuff. She pulls out felt horses, pixie officer uniforms, pixie convict handcuffs, pixie circus elephants.

"Did the pixies see Donny set the fire?" I ask.

"No." She scowls like I've suggested beheading Santa Claus.

My stomach growls. The lemon cake is good. I wonder if Janet is going to eat her slice.

"Donny got paid," Janet whispers.

My mouth freezes, mid-bite. "What do you mean he got paid?" I ask. "For setting the fire?"

"The pixies say yes."

I snap my jaw shut. "Who paid Donny for setting the fire?"

Janet gallops her horses around the new pixie house.

Suddenly, the missing fifty dollars that Bea accused Jimmy of stealing floats through my head. My eyes are riveted to Janet.

"Do the pixies know who paid Donny?" I ask.

Janet nods ever so slightly.

My mouth is so dry, I can hardly speak. "Was it your dad?" my voice croaks. "Did he steal the fifty dollars from the store to pay Donny?"

"He didn't *steal*! It's our money. He just forgot to tell my mom." Janet's pixie horses stop galloping. She shoves them helter-skelter back in the pixie house shoe box.

"The pixies said that, not me," she informs the floor. Her

shoulders are low like the pixie house weighs a ton as she carries it out the door.

I can hardly breathe. I couldn't have heard what I thought I heard. I head straight for my parents' room. "Dad, I have to talk to you *now*."

My father's eyes are closed, his head sunk into the pillow. "What?" He blinks his hazy eyes.

"You got to hear this."

He pulls himself up to a sitting position.

His frown deepens as I tell him what Janet said. He tips his head to the side and pulls his lips in away from my words. "I can't believe that," he says.

"It makes sense, though."

"A lot of things make sense that aren't true," he says. "Let's not jump to conclusions. All we know for sure is a seven-year-old child's imaginary friends have come up with a theory."

"Come on, Dad, Janet must have heard her parents talking about this."

My father's eyes are focused out the door. "She's a fanciful child. That may be all there is to this."

"Dad, I think it's true."

"Then Donny's lawyer will bring it up. He'll use it to plea-bargain a shorter sentence."

"But what about Darby?"

"If it comes out in court, then Darby will be charged." My father is reaching for his jacket. He runs a comb through his hair.

"Where are you going?"

"I'm gonna talk to Warden Williams about this right now."

"You do think it's true."

"I think it warrants further examination."

"But Dad, why would Darby pay Donny to set fire to our apartment?"

My father takes in a sharp breath. "In Darby's mind, I'm the threat. He feels the cons are here to be punished and my plans to rehabilitate them are crazy at best, dangerous at worst. I would never compromise when it comes to safety, but he doesn't see it that way."

"He figured Natalie would be charged with the fire and we'd be asked to leave?"

"Maybe he believed he was doing the world a favor. He's never thought Natalie belonged on the island. Look, let's take this one step at a time, Moose. We don't know if any of this is true. Right now, you need to honor your commitment to Janet and keep quiet."

"Okay," I say as I watch him leave.

Even now, hearing what Trixle may have done to us, my father is fair, thoughtful, and even-tempered. This is why he is the warden and Trixle is not.

29. Al Capone Drops the Ball

Saturday, February 29, 1936

Things will be changing tomorrow and we all know it. The cons have finally finished the work on #2E, so I will no longer be living half my life up top, the other half in 64 building. Natalie will be back at the Esther P. Marinoff during the week and Piper will be going to boarding school. It took a while for the warden to work out a deal with the FBI and then locate a school that would take Piper in the middle of the year, but it's all settled now. After tomorrow, we won't see her except for holidays and summers. We'll all miss her, even if she is a pain in the butt a lot of the time.

Annie and Piper, Jimmy, Theresa, Natalie, and me are all at the Mattamans' like always. We're trying to hold on to the old life, even as it's slipping away. It's hard to believe things are changing this much.

"What's the name of the school you're going to?" Jimmy asks.

"St. Ignatius School for Girls," Piper says.

"Is it a nunnery?" he asks.

"No," she laughs.

"So whatever happened about the money?" Annie wants to know.

Piper shrugs. "I owe two hundred and eighty-five dollars. Gotta pay it all back."

"Two hundred and eighty-five dollars . . . how are you going to get that kind of money?" Annie asks.

"Babysitting," Piper says.

"You're going to be a grandma by the time you make two hundred and eighty-five dollars babysitting," Jimmy tells her.

I think Piper will get mad at this, but she just shrugs. "I had another idea, but it didn't work out."

"What was that?" I ask.

Piper leans down to her book bag, takes out a baseball, and hands it to me.

I turn it over. Carved into the leather in awkward hatch-mark strokes are the words *Do your own time.*

"What's that supposed to mean?" I ask.

"Thought I might get a little help from Capone. I threw the ball over the rec yard wall with a note asking him to sign it for me. Do you know how much a baseball signed by Al Capone is worth?"

"A lot," I say.

"So wait, Al Capone wrote *Do your own time*?" Annie asks.

"Yeah," Piper says.

"Funny guy," I say.

"C'mon, all he had to do was sign one stupid baseball. His signature is worth more than FDR's."

"Why would a gangster's signature be worth more than the president's?" Annie asks.

"Same reason David Hughes isn't as famous as Machine Gun Kelly," Jimmy points out.

"Who is David Hughes?" I ask.

"He invented the radio," Jimmy says.

"Never heard of him," I say.

"That's the point," Jimmy says.

"Hey," Piper says as she peers out the Mattamans' front window. "Look who's down at the dock . . . the devil himself."

Sure enough, there is Donny Caconi in a gray pinstriped suit helping his mom carry suitcases and boxes from her apartment.

"Mrs. Caconi is moving out?" I ask.

"Going to live with her sister in Fort Bragg," Annie says.

"Be the last time you'll ever see Donny, that's for sure. Unless of course they send him to prison here," Piper says.

"Hey, you know, you're right." Jimmy dashes to his room and comes out with a small paper sack.

"He's out on bail, isn't he?" Piper asks.

"I thought he was broke. How'd he get the money together for bail?" I ask.

"He's Donny Caconi, that's how. I mean, how did he know the Count? How did the Count trust him with the locker number and combination? He has connections, that's how," Piper says.

"C'mon, Moose," Jimmy says. "We got business with Donny."

"We do?" I ask.

Jimmy turns and looks at me. "I never did think he beat you fair and square. Did you?"

Heat rises in my face. This is not the kind of thing I want to admit.

Jimmy smiles. "That's what I figured. Now, c'mon."

"If you think Donny Caconi will ever tell you the truth about anything, you're wrong," Piper says.

"Yeah, we know. C'mon, Natalie," Jimmy says.

"One thing that doesn't make sense is why the Count needs money," I tell Jimmy as we head down the stairs with Natalie. "He's in prison for life."

"His daughter needed money. And he wanted to give her the real stuff. Besides, it's pretty boring in prison. Conning people is like, you know, his hobby."

Down at the dock, Jimmy pulls out a few bottle caps from his sack.

Donny ignores us as he carries a small trunk from his mom's apartment to the dock.

Jimmy walks right up to Donny. "It's the weight," he tells Donny, holding out the bottle caps. "Makes all the difference. The light one here is harder to throw. The heavy one goes farther. But when you change the shape just slightly—make it more aerodynamic—that helps too."

"But if they're too heavy," I take over, "that's a problem too, isn't it? You got to get it just right, don't you?"

Donny gives us a lazy shrug. All of his attention is on Natalie. "She's an interesting person, your sister," he tells me. "People think she can't do much, but she has a genius for numbers. Nobody expects her to understand much of anything . . . that's the beauty of it. Could do a lot with a person like that."

Natalie's standing by herself. She takes her own air space with her everywhere she goes, but Donny breaks through. He's talking to her now. I can tell from the careful way she's tipping her toe that she likes what he says. I walk over there, ready to bust him in the chops. I don't like Donny trying to charm her.

But Nat looks at Donny straight in the peepers. "Alcatraz three hundred and seventeen," she says.

What's she talking about? Nat is up to thirty-two in looking people in the eyes, not three hundred and seventeen.

Then it registers. This is the number of the next convict to arrive on Alcatraz.

"Gonna be your new prison number," I tell him.

Donny's eyes shift. He squirms like his clothes don't fit so well anymore.

"Alcatraz three hundred and seventeen," Nat repeats.

"Will you tell her to shut up?" Donny says.

But I don't tell her to shut up. When it comes to numbers, Natalie never makes a mistake.

Author's Note

"On the Island there is a man who keeps the outside in touch."

In researching Alcatraz Island in the 1930s, I came across a letter addressed to the first warden on Alcatraz, James A. Johnston. The letter contained this sentence: "On the Island there is a man who keeps the outside in touch." There was nothing in the files that revealed what exactly this letter was referring to, who this mysterious person might be, or if there was any truth to this allegation, but I could not get that unsettling phrase out of my mind. As a novelist, I know that obsession is a blessing, and four years later the phrase that burned a hole in my head became the book you have in your hands.

That one sentence may have triggered the writing, but many ideas and more than ten years of background research have come together to create this story. The second idea came from a comment I heard on Alcatraz Alumni Day, which is held every year on the second weekend of August. I have attended almost every Alcatraz Alumni Day since 1998, the year I worked on the island to research the book. I've had the good fortune to speak to many former guards, convicts, and kids who grew up on the island. During one Alumni Day, I heard that in the thirties, fire escapes did not exist in 64 building, where many of the families of guards lived. Though there were no serious fires on the island, it made me wonder what could have happened if there had been.

Another idea came while researching a convict named Robert Miller, Alcatraz #300, who arrived on the island in 1936. Robert Miller, one of the world's most infamous con men, had some forty-five aliases, the best-known of which was Count Victor Lustig. Most of the facts about his long and preposterous criminal history that Annie and Theresa placed on the convict card are true to the best of my knowledge. By posing as a French government official, he was able to sell the Eiffel Tower "repeatedly."[1] After stealing money from bankers, he did convince them that it was not in their best interest to press charges. And then he "insisted that they should give him $1,000 for the inconvenience the arrest had caused him." [2]

One of the Count's favorite cons involved the sale of his money box. He had many of these wooden boxes made, complete with a false bottom and multiple impressive-looking dials. The box, he claimed, could reproduce money for you.[3]

Lustig would turn the cranks that would feed a real twenty-dollar bill and a piece of good paper into the box. He then claimed the bill would need to soak in a chemical bath for six hours in order to be imprinted with the correct image. At the end of that time, he would crank out two perfect twenty-dollar bills, both of which were real. One was the original bill, the other was a bill the Count had placed in the fake bottom.

---

1 DUANE SWIERCZYNSKI, ***The Complete Idiot's Guide to Frauds, Scams, and Cons*** (Indianapolis: Alpha, 2003), 187

2 www.uselessinformation.org. The only source for this is a website, so I'm not one hundred percent certain this is true.

3 DUANE SWIERCZYNSKI, ***The Complete Idiot's Guide to Frauds, Scams, and Cons*** (Indianapolis: Alpha, 2003), 187

The Count then sold his money box for $4,000 to $46,000.[4] By the time his victim had waited the requisite six hours and realized the box was a hoax, the Count had vanished.

What interests me most about this scheme is the fact that the mark was complicit. Of course, duplicating money in any form is against the law. That idea found its way into the fictional laundry caper. Piper knew it was wrong. Neither Annie Bomini nor Moose Flanagan would have fallen for this con. The best protection against being conned is common sense.

The Count was known to keep his counterfeiting materials in lockers.[5] Prior to his time on Alcatraz, the Count was even successful at conning Al Capone, by using a double-your-money scam. Even though Capone knew Count Lustig was a con man, when the Count came to him offering to double his money, Capone took the offer and handed the Count $50,000. A few months later the Count returned to tell Capone he had been unsuccessful at doubling Capone's money. Capone was furious. He was about to set his gorillas loose on the Count, sure he had run off with his $50,000, when the Count calmly returned all of his money. Capone was so relieved to see his beloved $50,000 that when the Count asked for $5,000 for his trouble, Capone was happy to hand it over. This was the Count's plan all along.[6]

That's a classic Count Lustig con. He would do an apparently nice thing, thus ingratiating himself to his victim. And then

---

4 DUANE SWIERCZYNSKI, *The Complete Idiot's Guide to Frauds, Scams, and Cons* (Indianapolis: Alpha, 2003), 187

5 *The New York Times,* August 31, 1949. "Lustig, 'Con Man,' Dead Since 1947."

6 DUANE SWIERCZYNSKI, *The Complete Idiot's Guide to Frauds, Scams, and Cons* (Indianapolis: Alpha, 2003), 186

once he had secured the victim's trust, he would ask for money. Count Lustig did not, to my knowledge, pull any cons on Alcatraz. According to his file at the National Archives in San Bruno, he spent his time on Alcatraz working in the laundry, taking correspondence courses, and writing a plan for world peace. It is true, however, that his real-life daughter, Mrs. Betty Jean Miller, was in desperate need of money[7] and the Count was unable to provide her with the cash she needed. Lustig was broke. He died in prison in 1947.

One of the most intriguing parts of researching Alcatraz is just when you think you've heard it all, some new story surfaces. A new nonfiction book on Alcatraz totally makes my day. In former Alcatraz guard Jim Albright's book he says that after lockdown at night some prisoners used cockroach messengers to trade cigarettes. "An inmate in one cell would catch a cockroach and tie a cigarette to its back with a piece of thread. The inmate a few cells down would place a piece of bread outside his cell knowing the cockroach would run for it."[8]

Though the character Donny Caconi is entirely fictional, his cons were inspired by the handiwork of Titanic Thompson—a con man working during the 1930s. Titanic's exploits included marking cards with his pinkie nail, using "dirty" dice, dealing from the bottom while misdirecting attention with a coughing attack. He often worked in tandem with supposed strangers "planted" in a situation but dressed to look like country bumpkins. During one con, he tried to hustle Al Capone by filling a lemon with buckshot and planting it in a

7 Count Lustig's file, National Archives, San Bruno, CA

8 JIM ALBRIGHT, *Last Guard Out: A Riveting Account by the Last Guard to Leave Alcatraz* (Bloomington, IN: AuthorHouse, 2008), 103, 104

vendor's fruit cart. He then bet Capone $500 he could fling the lemon onto a nearby roof. But Capone was wise to him. He bought his own lemon, squashed it flat, then asked Ti to throw that one. Titanic was never on Alcatraz, but he probably should have been.

And of course it's true the kids lived on Alcatraz because their fathers were guards or electricians or wardens on the island. The warden preferred having his guards live on Alcatraz, as a quick response to an escape or uprising would not have been possible had his guards lived across the bay. It's also true that many people in San Francisco didn't believe kids or teens lived on the island. The stories abound of reactions people had to this information. Certainly a driver's license or a check with the address Alcatraz Island would get the attention of whoever saw it.

And yes, Al Capone was a prisoner and Warden Johnston did call him his "star boarder."[9] People thought Capone had his hand in everything. On Alcatraz "Capone retained star quality. The director of the Bureau of Prisons James Bennett called him 'the most prominent gangster of all time.' "[10] Capone loved the attention and fanned the flames of his celebrity. It's also true that when Al got mad at another con on Alcatraz, his only recourse was to scratch his name off his magazine subscription circulation sheet.

As always, there are differing accounts of what happened on the island depending on who you talk to. I have heard

9 JAMES A. JOHNSTON, *Alcatraz Island Prison and the Men Who Live There* (Douglas/Ryan Communication, 1999, 2001), 30

10 ROBERT J. SCHOENBERG, *Mr. Capone: The Real—and Complete—Story of Al Capone* (New York: William Morrow and Company, 1992), 337

numerous versions of the rules for the kids who lived in 64 building when the cons were working on the dock. There were, no doubt, different rules at different times in the twenty-nine years that Alcatraz was a working penitentiary. Each resident's experience was also a little different. Some residents, for example, had more contact with the cons than others. "Although it was uncommon, there were some unavoidable instances when a resident would come in contact with an inmate. One former resident recalled an occasion when he had thrown a ball over a link fence, and an inmate passed it back a few days later. Another remembered an incident when an inmate was tending a garden, and left a small flower bouquet with a perfectly tied ribbon made from a vine on a cement step."[11] Other things seemed to be consistent. There is widespread agreement that there was just one phone for all of 64 building, for example. The fact that the cons did the laundry for everyone on the island is also settled history.

I do try to stick to the facts about Alcatraz as much as possible. That said, the books are clearly fiction. The Flanagans, the Mattamans, the Bominis are all made up. And though Al Capone and Count Lustig were on the island in 1936, the date of the Count's arrival on Alcatraz is actually a few months later in 1936 than I have accounted for in this novel. And of course the Count and Capone could hardly have had conversations with fictional characters. Most of the other cons are also made up, although I did hear a story about a convict who ate a lizard, so that part may be true. The points game is fictional; however, the idea came from a convict named Jimmy Lucas, Alcatraz

11 MICHAEL ESSLINGER, *Alcatraz: A Definitive History of the Penitentiary Years* (San Francisco: Oceanview Publishing, 2003), 125

#224, who stabbed Al Capone in the basement of the cell house.[12] Many think Jimmy's goal was to earn bragging rights. He wanted to be known as the toughest guy on Alcatraz, the man who downed Al Capone.

The title *Al Capone Does My Homework* came from a student at Tenakill Middle School in Closter, New Jersey. His School Media Specialist, Brenda Kahn, sent me the title a number of years ago. I loved the title but had no intention of using it. The original title for this book was *Al Capone Is My Librarian*. After his stint in the laundry, Al worked as a janitor, mopping up the cell house, and then as the cell house librarian.[13] Though I loved the idea of Librarian Capone, I could not get it to work in the book. Little did I know this student's homework title idea would become a big part of the novel. I wish I could thank him or her in person!

In early revisions of this manuscript, Moose's homework assignment was a throwaway line. But one day I happened to be reading a biography of FDR when I came upon this paragraph: "In the end, he was so successful in shouldering aside his handicap and leading an active life, he gave the impression that he had no disability. Years later, when he became president, many Americans did not fully realize that Franklin Roosevelt could not use his legs. As Roosevelt struggled to walk, his wife and his mother were battling over his future. Sara [FDR's mother] was sure she knew what was best for Franklin. She believed that his career was finished,

---

12 MICHAEL ESSLINGER, ***Alcatraz: A Definitive History of the Penitentiary Years*** (San Francisco: Oceanview Publishing, 2003), 147

13 MARK DOUGLAS BROWN, ***Capone: Life Behind Bars*** (San Francisco: Golden Gate National Parks Conservancy, 2004), 33

that he should retire to the comfortable privacy of Hyde Park."[14] Those words resonated, as it seemed to me that FDR's mother was trying to protect her son, just as Mrs. Flanagan tried to protect Natalie. And though FDR's disability was not the least bit like Natalie's, the battle to overcome was wholly the same.

14 RUSSELL FREEDMAN, ***Franklin Delano Roosevelt*** (Boston: Clarion Books, Houghton Mifflin Company, 1992), 56, 57

Acknowledgments

I would like to thank my two favorite Alcatraz researchers: Chuck Stucker and Michael Esslinger. Both men have spent years carefully and lovingly preserving the history of the island. And both have been extraordinarily generous sharing their findings with me. Chuck has a unique perspective on Alcatraz, as he grew up on the island. Michael brings top-drawer research skills to bear on everything he does. A special thanks to Phyllis Twinney, a former resident of Alcatraz, who has been so encouraging to me in my work. Thanks goes to John Cantwell and Lori Brosnan and the many Alcatraz rangers who have dedicated their professional lives to researching the island and sharing that history with its visitors. Especially, I would like to thank Lori, who invited me to volunteer on the island in 1998 and 1999. I would also like to thank the Alcatraz Alumni Association and the Alcatraz Island Family group for welcoming me into the fold and sharing their many insights into life on the island.

This book owes a debt of gratitude to George DeVincenzi and Jim Albright, former Alcatraz guards, for sharing their experiences on the island, and Robert Luke, for speaking so eloquently on his time as a prisoner on Alcatraz.

I would also like to thank the National Archives in San Bruno for allowing me access to the files of Al Capone and Count Lustig. And Tim Wilson and the team of dedicated librarians at the San Francisco History Center, who have helped me find all kinds of arcane information, including whether or not the San Francisco Hospital of 1936 had an elevator. (I moved the scene to the stairwell. I wasn't convinced they did.)

Thank you to the team at Penguin who have helped me craft a trilogy of books from years of research and a billion wild ideas.

Most of the credit should go to my editor, Kathy Dawson, who is both talented and tenacious. Thank you for all the time and energy you've put into helping me improve my work. Thank you for believing in me and in these books.

A special shout-out to the Penguin book reps. They are the reason you are holding this book in your hand. Specifically I would like to thank: Ev, Biff, Sheila, John, Colleen, Steve, Alex, Todd, Jill, Doni, Nicole D., Dawn, and Nicole W.

Special appreciation goes to my daughter, Kai, who shared her belly button storage technique with me, and my son, Ian, who reminds me that I can be altogether too helpful. And, most of all, I would like to thank my husband, Jacob, who supported my writing when it made absolutely no sense to do so.

Check out the first Tale from Alcatraz!

1. Devil's Island

Friday, January 4, 1935

Today I moved to a twelve-acre rock covered with cement, topped with bird turd and surrounded by water. Alcatraz sits smack in the middle of the bay—so close to the city of San Francisco, I can hear them call the score on a baseball game on Marina Green. Okay, not that close. But still.

I'm not the only kid who lives here. There's my sister, Natalie, except she doesn't count. And there are twenty-three other kids who live on the island because their dads work as guards or cooks or doctors or electricians for the prison like my dad does. Plus there are a ton of murderers, rapists, hit men, con men, stickup men, embezzlers, connivers, burglars, kidnappers and maybe even an innocent man or two, though I doubt it.

The convicts we have are the kind other prisons don't want. I never knew prisons could be picky, but I guess they can. You get to Alcatraz by being the worst of the worst. Unless you're me. I came here because my mother said I had to.

I want to be here like I want poison oak on my private parts. But apparently nobody cares, because now I'm Moose Flanagan, Alcatraz Island Boy—all so my sister can go to the Esther P. Marinoff School, where kids have macaroni salad in their hair and wear their clothes inside out and there isn't a chalkboard or a book in sight. Not that I've ever been to the Esther P. Marinoff. But all of Natalie's schools are like this.

I peek out the front window of our new apartment and look up to see a little glass room lit bright in the dark night. This is the dock guard tower, a popcorn stand on stilts where somebody's dad sits with enough firepower to blow us all to smithereens. The only guns on the island are up high in the towers or the catwalks, because one flick of the wrist and a gun carried by a guard is a gun carried by a criminal. The keys to all the boats are kept up there for the same reason. They even have a crapper in each tower so the guards don't have to come down to take a leak.

Besides the guard tower, there's water all around, black and shiny like tar. A full moon cuts a white path across the bay while the wind blows, making something creak and a buoy clang in the distance.

My dad is out there too. He has guard duty in another tower somewhere on the island. My dad's an electrician, for Pete's sake. What's he doing playing prison guard?

My mom is in her room unpacking and Natalie's sitting on the kitchen floor, running her hands through her button box. She knows more about those buttons than it seems possible to know. If I hide one behind my back, she can take one look at her box and name the exact button I have.

"Nat, you okay?" I sit down on the floor next to her.

"Moose and Natalie go on a train. Moose and Natalie eat meat loaf sandwich. Moose and Natalie look out the window."

"Yeah, we did all that. And now we're here with some swell fellows like Al Capone and Machine Gun Kelly."

"Natalie Flanagan's whole family."

"Well, I wouldn't exactly say they're family. More like next-door neighbors, I guess."

"Moose and Natalie go to school," she says.

"Yep, but not the same school, remember? You're going to this *nice* place called the Esther P. Marinoff." I try to sound sincere.

"*Nice* place," she repeats, stacking one button on top of another.

I've never been good at fooling Natalie. She knows me too well. When I was five, I was kind of a runt. Smallest kid of all my cousins, shortest kid in my kindergarten class and on my block too. Back then people called me by my real name, Matthew. Natalie was the first person to call me "Moose." I swear I started growing to fit the name that very day. Now I'm five foot eleven and a half inches—as tall as my mom and a good two inches taller than my dad. My father tells people I've grown so much, he's going to put my supper into pickle jars and sell it under the name Incredible Growth Formula.

I think about going in my room now, but it smells like the inside of an old lunch bag in there. My bed's a squeaky old army cot. When I sit down, it sounds like dozens of mice are dying an ugly death. There's no phonograph in this apartment. No washing machine. No phone. There's a radio cabinet, but someone yanked the workings out. Who gutted the radio, anyway? They don't let the criminals in *here* . . . do they?

So, I'm a little jumpy. But anybody would be. Even the silence here is strange. It's quiet like something you can't hear is happening.

I think about telling my best friend, Pete, about this place. "It's the Devil's Island . . . *doo, doo, doo.*" Pete would say in a deep spooky voice like they do on the radio. "Devil's Island . . . *doo, doo, doo,*" I whisper just like Pete. But without him it doesn't seem funny. Not funny at all.

Okay, that's it. I'm sleeping with my clothes on. Who wants to face a convicted felon in your pajamas?

And turn the page for a preview of the second Tale from Alcatraz

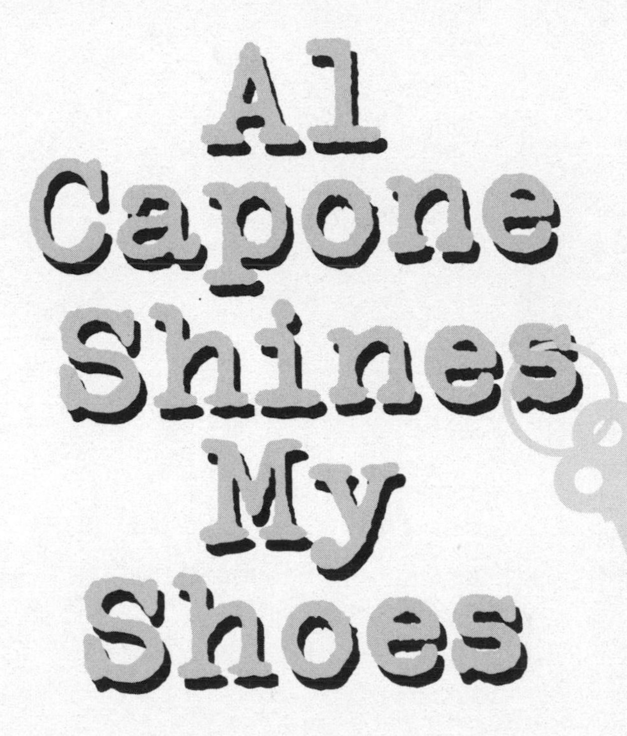

1. The Cream of the Criminal Crop

Monday, August 5, 1935

Nothing is the way it's supposed to be when you live on an island with a billion birds, a ton of bird crap, a few dozen rifles, machine guns, and automatics, and 278 of America's worst criminals—"the cream of the criminal crop" as one of our felons likes to say. The convicts on Alcatraz are rotten to the core, crazy in the head, and as slippery as eels in axle grease.

And then there's me. Moose Flanagan. I live on Alcatraz along with twenty-four other kids and one more on the way. My father works as a prison guard and an electrician in the cell house up top. I live where most of us "civilians" do, in 64 building, which is dockside on the east side of Alcatraz—a base hit from the mobster Al Capone.

Not many twelve-year-old boys can say that. Not many kids can say that when their toilet is stopped up, they get Seven Fingers, the ax murderer, to help them out, either. Even simple things are upside down and backwards here. Take getting my socks washed. Every Wednesday we put out our dirty laundry in big white bags marked with our name: FLANAGAN. Every Monday our clothes come back starched, pressed, folded, and smelling of soap and flour. They look like my mom washed them for me.

Except she didn't.

My laundry man is Alcatraz #85: Al Capone. He has help, of course. Machine Gun Kelly works right alongside him in the laundry along with thirty other no-name hit men, con men, mad dog murderers, and a handful of bank robbers too.

They do a good job washing the clothes for us and most everyone else on the island. But sometimes they do a little extra.

The cons don't care for Officer Trixle, so his laundry doesn't return the same way as everyone else's. His shirts are missing buttons, underwear is stiff with starch or dyed pansy pink, pants are missing a cuff or the fly is sewn shut so the guy can't even take a leak unless he pulls his pants down like a little girl.

I can't say the cons are wrong about Officer Trixle. Darby Trixle is the kind of guy who only his wife likes—and not that much either. Last Saturday my best friend Jimmy Mattaman and I were looking for a barrel for Jimmy's fly menagerie, and Janet Trixle, Darby's seven-year-old daughter, just happened to see we were walking by the Black Mariah, the Alcatraz paddy wagon. That was all we were doing—*walking by it*. But when Darby saw the Mariah had a flat tire, who do you think got the blame?

Yours truly.

It couldn't have been Darby drove over a nail. Oh no. It had to have been us. We had to go with him to San Francisco and carry a new tire down Van Ness Avenue, to the ferry and up the switchback, to where the Mariah was parked up top. Darby wouldn't even let us roll it on the road. Didn't want it to get dirty. It's a tire! Where does he think it usually goes?

My father wouldn't help us with Darby either. "I know you

had nothing to do with that flat tire, but it won't hurt you to give Darby a hand, Moose," is what he said.

When I first moved here, I thought all the bad guys were on one side of the bars and all the good guys were on the other. But lately, I've begun to wonder if there isn't at least one officer on the free side who ought to be locked up and maybe a convict who isn't half as bad as he's cracked up to be. I'm thinking about Al Capone—the most notorious gangster in America, the worst guy we have up top. How could it be that he did me a good turn?

It doesn't make sense, does it? But Al Capone got my sister, Natalie, into a school called the Esther P. Marinoff where she'd been turned down twice already. It's a boarding school for kids who have their wires crossed up. It's a school and not a school . . . a place to make her normal.

I don't know for certain it was Capone who helped us. I mean the guy is locked up in a five-by-nine-foot cell. He's not allowed to make a phone call or write a letter that isn't censored word for word. It doesn't seem possible he could have done anything to help us, even if he wanted to.

But out of desperation, I sent a letter asking Capone for help and Natalie got accepted. Then I got a note in the pocket of my newly laundered shirt: *Done,* it said.

I haven't told anyone about this. It's something I try not to think about, but today, the day Nat's finally leaving for school, I can't keep my mind from going over the details again and again.

The thing that stumps me is *why.* I never even met Al Capone . . . why would he help me?

■ ■ ■

I watch Nat as she sits on the living room floor going through our books one by one. She looks almost like a regular sixteen-year-old this morning, if her mouth wasn't twitching right and right and right again and her shoulders were just down where they're supposed to be. She opens a book, fans her face with the pages, then sets the book back on the shelf, just exactly as it was. She has been through one entire shelf this way. Now she's working on the second.

Normally, my mom wouldn't let her do this, but today she doesn't want to take the chance of upsetting her.

"You ready to go, Natalie?" my mother asks.

Nat moves faster. She fans the pages so quickly each book sounds like one quick *ffffrrrt*. All I hear is *ffffrrrt ffffrrrt ffffrrrt* as I look out our front window down to the dock. Sure enough there's Officer Trixle. He's supposed to be off today, but Trixle can't keep his nose out of our business. He's almost as much trouble as Piper, the warden's daughter—only not half as pretty. When you look like Piper does, people forgive a whole lot of things, but never mind about that. What I think about Piper is kind of embarrassing, to tell you the truth.

My father comes out of the bathroom. The toilet is running again. The plumbing in 64 building is held together with bubble gum and last year's oatmeal stuck hard and solid. But luckily for us, Seven Fingers, our very own felon plumber, fixes it for free. Not exactly for free actually. We pay him a chocolate bar every time, but no one is supposed to know that.

"Time to go, Natalie," my mom says.

Natalie is wearing a new yellow dress today. My mother cut the pattern, but the convicts in the tailor shop sewed it. The cons did a pretty good job. Only the belt is bugging Nat. She pulls at it, weaving it in and out of the loops. In and out. In and out. Nat's mouth puckers to one side. "Moose school. Natalie home," she says.

"Not today," my mother says brightly. "Today is your big day. Today *you're* going to school."

"*Not* today," Nat tells her. "*Not* today. *Not* today."

I can't help smiling at this. Natalie likes to repeat what you say and here she's repeating my mom's exact words with a change of inflection that makes them say what Natalie wants them to say and not at all what my mother meant. I love when Natalie outsmarts Mom this way. Sometimes Nat is smarter than we are. Other times, she doesn't understand the first thing about anything. That's the trouble with Natalie—you never know which way she'll go.

The first time Nat went to the Esther P. Marinoff School she pitched a fit the size of Oklahoma and they kicked her out, but I don't think that will happen this time. She's getting better in her own weird way. I used to say Nat's like a human adding machine without the human part, but now she's touching down human more days than not. And each time she does it feels as if the sun has come out after sixty straight days of rain.

"Tell her, Moose. Tell her how wonderful it's going to be," my mother says.

"Tell her, Moose. Tell her how wonderful it's going to be," Nat repeats, picking up her button box and holding it tight against her chest.

"You get to take your buttons, Nat. *Mom* said," I say.

I almost think I see her smile then—as much of a smile as

you ever get from Natalie anyway. She peeks inside her button box, checking to make sure all of her precious buttons are exactly where they're supposed to be.

When we head down to the dock, my mom's step is light on the stairs. She's so sure that the Esther P. Marinoff will be the thing that fixes Natalie. My dad's feet are moving to the beat of an Irish jig. Natalie is taking each step carefully and methodically as if she wants each foot to make a lasting impression on the stairs.

When we get down to the water's edge I see Trixle walking across the dock, bullhorn in hand.

"*Two hundred yards back please! All boats must stay two hundred yards off the shore!*" Officer Trixle booms through his bullhorn to a tour boat that has come too close to the island.

"Warned him before, that one. Mac'll put a bead on him. Fix 'em good," Trixle tells my father.

Natalie hates loud noises. Once they shot a warning blast into the water when we were in our apartment and she curled up in a ball in the middle of the living room and stayed that way for the better part of the afternoon. Another time she didn't seem to hear a gun go off ten feet away. It's impossible to predict what Natalie will do.

"Darby, hey Darby . . ." my father wheedles. "Please—not today, okay, buddy?"

"Got to learn to straighten up and fly right," Darby mutters, "if she's coming back, that is." His eyes are bright with the unasked question.

Before the tower guard can get the boat in his gun sights, it turns starboard and hightails back to the city, and the tick in my mom's cheek relaxes.

Officer Trixle gets a happy little bounce to his step. He motions to the guard tower anyway, and the guard tower officer pelts the bay with a showy spray of firepower that pounds like fireworks exploding inside your head.

Natalie shrieks high and piercing like the escape siren. She closes her eyes, wraps her arms around her head, and begins to rock.

The bullets don't get anywhere near the tour boat, but it roars forward, sinking low behind as it struggles to gain speed.

"Natalie, it's all done now. It's all over. No more guns, okay? No more," I tell her as my mother digs in her bag for the emergency lemon cake.

"They were leaving already," my mom whispers to my father. "That was completely unnecessary."

"He's just doing his job, Helen," my father says, but his face is pinched like his belt is a notch too tight.

Nat's arms stay wrapped around her head like a bandage. She rocks from foot to foot, still making her little shrieks.

Trixle hitches up his trousers and walks toward us. He stares at Natalie. "Got a problem here, Cam?"

"No problem. We got it under control." My father's voice is confident and commanding like a Boy Scout leader's.

Trixle sucks on his lip. "Don't look that way to me."

"Just scared her is all," my father tells him.

Trixle clears his throat. "Gonna have to do an incident report on this, Cam. Warden's orders."

My father frowns and lowers his voice as if he's letting Trixle in on a secret. "Nothing to worry about here, Darby."

Darby makes a juicy noise with his spit. "Anything out of the ordinary, I got to report."

My mom picks up Nat's suitcase, hoping to distract her and get her away from Darby. "Let's go, Nat," she says.

"But what about Jimmy and Theresa?" I ask. "They wanted to say goodbye. Couldn't you wait? I can run get them. It will only take a minute." Theresa is Jimmy's little sister and she's really good with Natalie.

My mom shakes her head. Nat's shrieking has subsided. Now it's more like the hum of a radio gone haywire. But my mom clearly wants to get her out of here.

I don't think Nat will go, but she does. She's still humming, still holding her head, but she's walking along behind my mother, yes she is.

"Bye, Nat." I wave stiffly.

"Moose bye. Moose bye," she says as she toe-walks across the gangplank.

I take a step forward. I know better than to try to hug her. Nat hates to be touched, but I want to go get the Mattamans at least. I promised I'd let them know when she was leaving.

My father puts his hand on my arm. "She can't take much more hullabaloo," he murmurs, his eyes on Darby Trixle, who is deep in conversation with the buck sergeant.

My mom waves to us from the starboard side, scooting Nat's suitcase under the seat. Nat sits down, her eyes trained on her lap. The motor roars to a start and the *Frank M. Coxe* pulls out fast, carving a white wake in the stirred-up brown water.

We watch until the boat is so small it could fit in the finger of my baseball glove. And then it's gone.